"Aren't you going to tell me your name?" he prompted as he held the car door.

"Starr," she replied as she turned the key in the ignition. "And if you're going to smoke, which aside from being bad for your health is polluting other people's air, you shouldn't throw the butts on the ground. Even if it is your ground."

For a minute he stared at her with a disbelieving look, and then broke into laughter as she pulled away.

"Of all the arrogant, despicable men I've ever met," she fumed to herself. But she had been almost hypnotized by those dazzling green eyes, lost in their mysterious depths. He was no doubt the most vibrantly alive man she had ever encountered.

Bittersweet Love

BETTY R. HEADAPOHL

LIVING BOOKS
Tyndale House Publishers, Inc.
Wheaton, Illinois

Second printing,, November 1986

Library of Congress Catalog Card Number 84-51664
ISBN 0-8423-0181-X, paper

CONTENTS

ONE
The
Stranger

As Starr climbed through the barbed wire fence, the sharp prongs caught one of her sneakers with a tenacious grip.

"Drat," she muttered as she wrestled her foot free. Pushing her straw hat back on her dark hair, she leaned over and inspected the ground with close scrutiny. On her hands and knees, she scanned the thick vegetation with an experienced eye. A few thrusts with the knife and she plopped a clump of greenery into her basket. Her braids bobbed up and down as she vigorously pursued her task. In a few minutes a thin layer of perspiration coated her neck and face.

She should have brought something to drink, she thought, as she licked her dry lips. She was intent on pulling a particularly deep-rooted plant when a soft laugh made her freeze.

"Well, well, what have we here?" a masculine voice drawled as she jumped to her feet, upsetting the basket. Starr flushed as she watched the tall blond man approaching her. Suddenly, she was acutely aware of her disheveled attire.

He stopped a few feet from her and leaned against an oak tree, casually lighting a cigarette.

Starr frowned her disapproval.

"You realize you're trespassing?" he asked as he slowly appraised her tall figure from behind his dark sunglasses.

Starr, burning from his arrogant scrutiny, snapped at him, "I'm not trespassing. I have permission from the owner to collect herbs here. What are you doing here?" she countered, drawing herself up haughtily to her full five feet nine inches.

"I, my lovely little wood nymph, am the new owner of this tract of land. And you're—" he coaxed.

Starr ignored his quest for her name. "I didn't know that the property had been sold. It only went up for sale last week." She was beginning to feel uneasy.

"That's when I bought it, my dear." He pointed to the "No Trespassing" sign which she had failed to notice. "And put that up."

With a guilty look, Starr glanced at her over-turned basket as he laughed in amusement.

"Caught you with the goods, didn't I?"

In defense she glared at his knowing smirk. Clad in well-worn denim jeans and a shirt tied around his waist, his deeply tanned chest and arms glistened in the hot sun. His thick, dark blond hair reminded her of a lion's mane.

"I'll pay you for these plants," she informed him as she raised her chin in defiance.

He moved suddenly with the grace of a large cat until he stood barely a foot from her. Despite the heat, a shiver traced its way up her spine as he removed his sunglasses and she gazed into the teasing depths of the greenest eyes she had ever seen. Her knees began to tremble as she stared at him speechlessly.

Frightened, Starr backed away from his threatening stance and stumbled over the forgotten basket. He reached out instinctively and caught her before she could fall.

As he held her, he studied the planes of her glowing, suntanned face. "I was right," he teased as she continued to gaze wordlessly into his impish eyes, "you are a wood nymph. And if I close my eyes, you'll probably disappear."

Suddenly, Starr regained her senses and jerked free of his supporting arms. The sun must have affected her brain, she thought as she grabbed her basket of herbs and glanced nervously around the deserted meadow. How did she know he was really the new owner of the Braden property? For all she knew he could be an escaped convict. Or worse. She cast a dubious glance at his blond hair. Not many men in the Springfield area would dare wear their hair that long. Although she had to admit it did go well with his rugged features.

"Here, my little wood nymph," he said as he reached down to retrieve her straw hat, which had fallen to the ground when she had stumbled.

Gently, he placed it on her dark hair. "Shall I hold the barbed wire for you or would you prefer to use the gate?" he asked, a mischievous sparkle lighting his eyes.

Attempting to regain her composure, Starr walked stiffly toward the gate. How did he know that she had crawled through the fence unless he'd been watching her? She heard him walking behind her and realized he was no doubt enjoying her discomfort.

He reached around her to open the gate. "Call me the next time you want to collect posies. I'm Trevor Hall and I'm staying at the Holiday Inn in Pixley until I find a place."

"They're herbs," she informed him disdainfully, ignoring his invitation.

He followed her down the road to where she had parked her little yellow Volkswagen. "Aren't you going to tell me your name?" he prompted as he held the car door.

"Starr," she replied as she turned the key in the ignition. "And if you're going to smoke, which aside from being bad for your health is polluting other people's air, you shouldn't throw the butts on the ground. Even if it is your ground."

For a minute he stared at her with a disbelieving look, and then broke into laughter as she pulled away.

"All right, Starr," he called after her. "I'll clean up my act."

Glancing in the rearview mirror, Starr saw he was still gazing after her departing car with an amused expression.

"Of all the arrogant, despicable men I've ever met," she fumed to herself. But she had been almost hypnotized by those dazzling green eyes, lost in their mysterious depths. He was no doubt the most vibrantly alive man she had ever encountered. She could still feel the strength of those hard, muscular arms. Slowly, Starr shook her head as though trying to blot away the image of those teasing eyes.

By the time she reached the health food store she owned and operated, her emotional equilibrium had been partially restored. She took down the "Out to Lunch" sign, unlocked the door, and glanced down Main Street. It was practically deserted. The heat was keeping everyone inside. Immediately she checked the upright freezer and sighed with relief when she saw it was working. She opened a bottle of cold grape juice and greedily devoured it before carrying the basket of herbs into the small room behind the shop. Rinsing the small green plants carefully, she placed them on paper towels to dry.

She heard the soft tinkling of the bell above the door and dried her hands.

"Hi, Jan. You must be the only person out today."

"I know," the small redhead agreed. "It must be over a hundred out there." She looked around for a chair. "I thought I'd come over and eat my lunch here with you. Anything to get out of that office! The air conditioner hasn't worked for a week." She settled herself into the plastic bucket chair as she kicked off her shoes and unwrapped her sandwich.

"Busy day?" Starr asked.

"Busy? Ever since the sale of the Braden property it's been busier than a long-tailed cat in a roomful of rocking chairs. Say, could I have some milk to wash this down?" She reached for her purse.

"Sure. Forget the money." Starr waited until Jan had taken a long drink of the cool liquid. "Why has the sale of that property made you so busy? And you never mentioned to me that it had been sold."

Jan's big brown eyes widened. "I thought I did. But anyway, the rumor is that the new owner's going to develop that tract into a housing subdivision. And everyone wants some of the action. Do you know what that could mean for the economy of this town?"

Starr's stomach gave a sickening lurch. "Sure," she began angrily. "I suppose he's going to cut down all the trees and put two thousand people in an area that should support only two hundred and call it progress. I'd like to see that land stay just as it is. There are enough scars already on the land from mining."

"Oh, Starr. You and your ecology. Just think of all the business you'd get if that became a housing development." Jan chewed her sandwich in thoughtful contemplation.

"Is that bologna, Jan?" Starr asked in an accusing tone.

"Well—er—yes. It's the only thing I had time to fix this morning," she admitted sheepishly. "I should have known your eagle eyes would spot it."

"You know that's filled with nitrites and chemical additives, plus some poor cow had to give its life for your lunch."

As Starr launched into her tirade, Jan finished her sandwich in a hurry in a hasty endeavor to destroy the evidence.

"Really, Jan! My best friend. I hope no one comes in and sees you eating a bologna sandwich!"

"Say," Jan interjected, ignoring Starr's nutrition lecture, "you ought to see this Trevor Hall, the new owner of the Braden property. Is he ever nice. And wealthy as Rockefeller, I hear."

"I think I have met him," Starr said dryly as she ripped open a case of soybeans and started pricing them.

"You what?"

Starr giggled at Jan's wide-eyed look. "He caught me trespassing on his property just a little while ago."

Jan continued to look at her in disbelief as she sipped her milk. "Trespassing?"

"Well," Starr said with an air of indignation, "I didn't know the property had been sold. My best friend never bothered to tell me. The Bradens had always let me gather herbs whenever I wanted."

"What did he say?"

"Not much," Starr said with a shrug as she tried to push away the memory of those teasing green eyes.

Jan snorted. "Not much. I bet he couldn't keep his eyes off of you. Just because you've shut yourself off from men for the last five years doesn't mean that they're blind."

"Indeed my eyes were glued to this gorgeous creature," a deep voice said from the doorway.

Jan and Starr jumped as the object of their conversation entered the store.

Indignant at his eavesdropping, Starr lashed out at him. "Do you always sneak around listening and watching other people?"

"Only when I can use it to my advantage, Miss Monroe."

So he had learned her last name. She continued to glare at him, wondering who had told him. His chest was now covered with a light green polo shirt that made the blond highlights gleam in the thick hair that tumbled past his collar.

Momentarily ignoring her outburst, he turned his attention to Jan. "Mrs. Stevens, if you would be so kind as to return to your office a little early and type the final papers for the transfer of my property, I would forever be in your debt."

What a line, Starr thought. Inwardly, she seethed at the way Jan immediately jumped to her feet, hastily shoved on her shoes, and headed across the street to do his bidding. Without looking up, she continued to price the soybeans with a vicious banging.

"Independent little cuss, aren't you?" he asked finally.

"Evidently you haven't noticed, Mr. Hall, but I'm not exactly little," she informed him through clenched teeth.

"Oh, I'd noticed," he assured her with an irritating smugness.

Anger spread wildly through her as she looked up to catch his disturbing gaze.

"Never cared much for small women," he continued in a lazy drawl.

"Like to pick on someone your own size?" she snapped as she slammed the last package of soybeans down on the counter.

"Yep."

Starr saw the twinkle in his eyes and broke into laughter despite herself.

"You have a lovely laugh, Starr Monroe."

Flustered, she looked down at the counter. "I guess we got off on the wrong foot, Mr. Hall," she admitted, offering her hand in apology.

"Trevor," he said as he took her hand and squeezed it once before reluctantly releasing it. "Let's start over, Starr Monroe. How about having dinner with me tonight?"

"I'd like that."

"Good. What time do you close your store?"

"Five, but—" she glanced down at her slacks, which she had donned in the back room.

"I have some appointments to keep. Why don't you come to my room at the Holiday Inn in Pixley when you're ready?"

Her dark eyebrows raised in a question mark as he laughed at her dubious expression.

"I'm an honorable man, Miss Monroe. If you don't trust me, you can call me from the lobby when you arrive."

Starr smiled at his immediate grasp of her thoughts. "I guess we small-town bumpkins are rather transparent, aren't we?"

He chuckled. "See you tonight, Starr."

She watched him walk across the street with a lithe grace that reminded her again of a big tawny cat. A lot of hearts were going to beat faster in Springfield—of that she was very sure.

After work she hurried down the back road toward home, a knot tightening in her stomach. It had been a long time since she had dated anyone. Actually, she mused, she couldn't remember ever dating anyone quite like Trevor Hall.

Searching frantically through her closet, she glanced in the mirror at her hair. Should she take time to wash it? No, if she did it would have to be blow-dried and then it would be frizzy. She discarded item after item in a huge heap on the bed until she was a bundle of nerves. At last she decided on a powder blue sleeveless dress and white heels—her highest ones. Tonight she could comfortably wear heels as high as she wanted.

She touched her wrists and throat with the expensive perfume Jan had bought her for Christmas. She pulled her long hair back into a sleek ponytail and added small ivory earrings. Simple, but it would have to do. Even before Kevin, she hadn't been the type to spend time in front of the mirror.

The afternoon sun still held a lot of fury as she drove the few short miles to the Holiday Inn in Pixley.

"Too bad I don't have air conditioning in this little bug," she muttered as she tried to rearrange her linen dress so it wouldn't look as if she had slept in it by the time she got to the hotel. She drove slower than usual to keep her hair from loosening in the wind as it blew warm against her face. A few loose strands fluttered freely around her moist temples, despite her efforts.

As Starr pulled the little yellow car into the hotel parking lot, she glanced down with dismay at the wrinkles in her dress. Brushing past the inquisitive desk clerk, she headed for the restroom. The cool interior of the hotel lobby was an immense relief after the heat of the humid drive. She pushed the errant strands of hair back in place as best she could, took a deep breath, and approached the desk clerk.

"Mr. Trevor Hall's room," she requested in as crisp a manner as she could muster.

"Room 503."

She felt as though his eyes were following her as she walked to the elevator. When the doors finally slid open, she stepped inside with a sigh of relief. Alone in the elevator, she clutched her purse to her chest. Meeting a strange man in his hotel room wasn't something she did every day. In the solitary surroundings of the enclosed car, she smiled to herself. Who was she kidding? Starr Monroe was the prototype of Small Town, USA . . . and glad of it.

As the doors glided open, she peered into the silent corridor. The thick red-and-black-flowered carpet muffled the sound of her footsteps as she moved silently down the dimly lit hallway. At the door, she hesitated before knocking. Perhaps she should go back downstairs to the lobby and wait for him to join her there. No, she decided, and squaring her shoulders, she rapped on the door with a confidence she didn't feel.

Instantly, Trevor appeared at the door, knotting a blue-and-gray tie. Her eyes dropped to the light blue silk shirt that suited his trim torso.

With amusement he glanced at her blue dress. "I see we've chosen the same color."

Starr smiled and gazed around the plush suite. "I only have two dresses. The other one's blue, too."

Laughing softly at her candor, he steered her to the sofa. "May I say you look as lovely in your dress as you do in your denims?" His eyes twinkled with a mischievous gleam that lit their green depths.

It was on the tip of her tongue to tell him he was as attractive shirted as he was bare-chested, but she found his nearness too disturbing to chance commenting on his attire or lack of it earlier in the day.

"I'll be just a moment, Starr. Would you like a drink while you wait?"

Her black eyebrows lifted in disapproval. "Alcohol?"

"Uh, oh," he said in feigned dismay. "Is that in the same category as cigarettes?"

"Just as bad for your health," she informed him. "And the Bible constantly warns against its use."

His green eyes traveled over her tall, well-proportioned figure. "Well, you're certainly a walking advertisement for your store. You're the healthiest-looking woman I've ever seen."

Flushing from his compliment, Starr lowered her eyes and pretended to study the pattern in the hotel carpet. A few minutes later he returned from the other room. He had added a light-weight gray suit jacket.

"Ready?"

She nodded and stood up. "Where are we going?" she asked as he took her arm.

"The desk clerk told me about a nice little Italian restaurant in Johnson City. I thought we'd try that."

"Johnson City! That's over fifty miles from here."

"I guess that's what happens when you live in California too long. You don't think anything about driving that far for dinner." He glanced at her stern profile. "You do eat something besides soybeans and sprouts?" He raised a quizzical eyebrow.

"Pasta is fine, but I don't eat animal flesh."

He groaned as he shut the hotel door behind them and dropped the key into his pocket. "How long have you been a health food—" He stopped in embarrassment.

"Nut?" she finished for him as the elevator began its descent. "Ever since I graduated from college. I started out to be a dietician, but I disbelieved so many of the things I was being taught that I decided to learn all I could about the subject on my own."

Trevor unlocked the door of a white Cadillac and helped her into the front seat.

As he slid behind the wheel, she asked, "Don't

you feel guilty polluting the air with this big monster? It's a diesel, isn't it?"

"No, I don't; and yes, it is." He looked over his shoulder and backed the large car out of the parking space with ease. "I suppose you're the head of the local chapter of the EPA?"

Their eyes locked in direct combat.

"I have to breathe the air you're polluting."

They argued about pollution nearly all the way to Johnson City. After they were seated in the small Italian restaurant, Starr questioned him about the housing project.

Trevor lit a cigarette and caught her look of disapproval.

"Have you ever seen a cancerous lung?" she asked in an ominous tone.

"I know. Don't quote to me. The Bible says the body is a temple. Good grief, lady, you're impossible," he said as he snuffed out the cigarette in the small, crystal ashtray. "Is it all right if I drink my water?"

"Suits me. It was your idea to ask me to dinner."

Seeing the flash of fire in her bright blue eyes, he quickly changed the subject.

"How come a beautiful girl like you isn't married, Starr?"

She stared down at her unadorned hands.

"Starr?" he whispered as she lifted her sad blue eyes in answer.

"Isn't it obvious? You're already disliking me. I'm always on my soapbox about something, I guess."

"You certainly never could be accused of being apathetic. But somehow I have a vision of you with a loving husband, a houseful of kids, all with that gorgeous black hair and those blue eyes." He laughed. "I can see all of those little heads around the table eating your homemade bread and peanut butter."

She flushed and looked down at the silverware.

"Is that a blush from Miss Emancipated?"

"I'll have to hurry to have the houseful of kids. I'll be twenty-eight this December."

"Practically over the hill," he teased. "Tell me, Starr," he asked, reaching across the table and taking her hand in his, "why is it some lucky guy isn't coming home to your waiting arms and sprout sandwiches every night?"

In the candlelit glow of the small restaurant, she raised her large blue eyes and he was surprised to see tears glistening.

"I'll never get married," she whispered.

"Never?" He searched her face for a long moment, not finding any clue.

"'Once burned, twice shy,'" she quoted cryptically and tried to smile brightly at the waiter bringing their orders. Slowly, she savored the Fettucini Alfredo before turning the tables on him. "Why aren't you married? Wealthy, handsome, charming. Sometimes," she added under her breath.

"Maybe I am." He winked as he lifted his wine glass.

She glanced at his bare left hand.

"I don't like rings."

"Most men don't," she agreed acidly.

He laughed at her sour observation. "Because most men wear them through their noses."

She studied his ruggedly handsome face. "I can't see you in that position."

"I never could either. That's why I'm not married."

She bristled at his arrogance. "All marriages aren't like that."

He smiled without comment, his green eyes silently denying the veracity of her statement.

Inwardly, she was trembling. She found him to be the most disturbing man she had ever met. Those cool green eyes missed nothing. She decided to explore a safer subject.

"Are you going to develop the Braden property into single-family dwellings?"

"I take it you don't approve of such a plan?"

Starr sighed. "It's such a beautiful place. For as long as I can remember, I've always gone there. I hate to see it filled with people." Her eyes grew sad. "Someday this country will be nothing but high-rise apartments from coast to coast. And everyone will have to wear gas masks when they venture out. We're so lucky here in West Virginia. Most of the land is still untouched because of the rough terrain."

"I think you're exaggerating. All I've heard lately is how West Virginia is losing its backward image, moving ahead to become an industrial leader. You certainly don't express that hope. I intend to develop only a few hundred acres. I can't see anything wrong with bringing some much-needed employment and competitively priced housing to this area. From what I've seen, Springfield could certainly benefit from it." His eyes had grown dark with a dangerous glint.

"I just hate to see that beautiful area destroyed—the trees, the serenity. Why can't you leave it as it is?" Her eyes pled with him to understand her innate feelings about the land she loved so dearly.

"Because I can't stay in business that way."

"That's the bottom line, isn't it?" she accused him in a bitter tone. "Money."

"Isn't that why you have your store?" His voice had grown cold. "I'm not going to let anyone make me feel guilty about making an honest profit."

"I'm in business, but I pride myself on thinking more about helping people than robbing their pocketbooks," she declared hotly, throwing down her napkin in disgust. She should never have accepted a dinner invitation from this profiteer.

"You don't care about making a profit? I find it hard to believe that you run that little store on a purely altruistic basis." He was barely controlling his temper.

"As a Christian, my primary goal is to help others. The almighty dollar isn't the most important thing in the world to me. You've got a lot to learn about people around here, Trevor Hall."

He shoved his plate back and signaled the waiter for the check. "I should have known you were an unreasonable little hillbilly when I first saw you today."

Starr turned white as she fought to control the rage about to explode in her. "Don't you ever call me a hillbilly again, Mr. Hall, you—you—fruit-and-nut Californian."

They didn't speak on the long drive back to Pixley. Starr looked out the window at the dark countryside. *Lord, forgive me for losing my temper again*, she prayed silently. *This man brings out the worst in me. How could such an appealing person be so pig-headed and blind?*

Trevor made no further attempts at conversation but kept his eyes on the road. As soon as he pulled into the nearest parking space in the hotel parking lot, Starr hopped out of his car and headed for her VW. But she was so upset she couldn't get the door to open. He reached around her and opened it, which only further infuriated her.

"Thank you for a most stimulating and enlightening evening, Miss Monroe."

"Just consider it your introduction to hillbilly hospitality," she snapped in return.

Laughing softly, he grasped her firmly by the upper arms. Starr looked around the deserted hotel lot as she tried in vain to pull away from him.

"Since I'm so profit-minded, I expect a return on my evening's investment," he said as he lowered his head to claim her lips. She tried to struggle, but his powerful hands held her immobile. For a fleeting moment she thought of screaming, but his lips silenced her protests.

Suddenly, Starr found herself responding to his kiss. The hands that had seconds before pushed against him in a bid for freedom now curled around his lean waist. Vaguely aware of the fresh, clean aroma of his after-shave, she returned his kiss with an ardor that surprised and shocked her.

When he released her, she looked up at him with dazed eyes.

"Not a bad yield," he commented caustically as he turned on his heel and strode away into the hotel entrance.

Stunned, Starr leaned against her car for a moment, wondering what had just happened to her. When his parting statement registered, her temper erupted. She slammed the door and started the motor. In her anger she let the clutch out too quickly and the little yellow VW hiccuped a few feet and died. It was a fitting finale for a miserable evening. She put her head down on the steering wheel and burst into tears.

She was still sniffling when she coasted into her driveway several minutes later.

TWO
A Picnic

"You had a date with that delectable man and you wound up fighting with him? Oh, Starr, I don't believe you."

"That 'delectable' man called me a hillbilly."

Jan's brown eyes widened in amazement as she shook her head in disbelief. "Well, you are. So am I." She poured another cup of coffee and wiped a crumb from the red-and-white-checked tablecloth.

Starr sipped her herb tea and grimaced. "It was the way he said it," she murmured angrily, recalling his icy expression. "He's a snob. A big city slicker. I hope he takes his money and his housing project and goes back to California with his progressive ideas."

Jan smiled at Starr's outburst. "Well, I don't. I think—" Whatever she was going to say was interrupted by the appearance of her three-year-old daughter, Melissa.

"Well, good morning, sleepyhead. What are you doing up so early?"

Starr watched the tousled redhead snuggle up in her mother's lap. Recalling Trevor Hall's statement about envisioning her with a houseful of kids, she smiled.

"What's so funny?" Jan asked as she tried to smooth her daughter's incorrigible curls into some kind of order.

"Nothing. Just thinking about what a good mother you are."

Starr saw the shadow of submerged grief pass across Jan's eyes and knew she was thinking of Frank. It didn't seem possible that he had been gone for two years—killed in a head-on collision on a rainswept mountain road when Melissa was only a year old.

"Starr, are you sure you don't mind watching these two all day? This is your only day away from the store. I can always drive up to Huntington to visit Charlotte some other time. I don't want you missing church on my account."

"Go," Starr ordered as she took Melissa from Jan and nestled her soft baby warmth in her arms. "And don't worry. I'll take good care of them."

She carried Melissa into the living room and they watched cartoons as Jan prepared for her trip to Huntington. Frank, Jr., staggered out of the bedroom crying as he realized his mother was leaving without him. His rumpled pajamas and disheveled hair completed the picture of early morning misery.

Watching Jan vacillate in the doorway, Starr

waved her away and coaxed Frank onto the couch, cuddling him under her other arm. Jan slipped away quietly, closing the door with a soft click.

Starr thought of Trevor again later when both children were looking suspiciously at the oatmeal she had prepared for them.

"I want Cap'n Crunch," Melissa wailed. Frank trailed his spoon wearily through his bowl, watching the pattern spread from side to side with an apathetic gaze.

Starr frowned as she inspected the contents of Jan's pantry. Nothing but presweetened cereals. No wonder the children were often so petulant with all that sugar in them!

"Your mother is a junk food junkie," she informed them as she slammed the cupboard door shut.

Frank stuck out his tongue at Melissa, who immediately broke into tears.

"Franklin Stevens, eat your oatmeal and quit tormenting your sister."

"It needs sugar," he insisted with a belligerent bang of his spoon on the table.

A headache was beginning to throb over her left temple. It looked like another hot day, and Jan wouldn't be back until late. **Trevor Hall, you're insane**, she thought. **A houseful? Two were more than sufficient.**

"No, it doesn't, Frank. Here," she said triumphantly, "let me put some of this on it." She squeezed the liquid honey on his oatmeal. "Now try it," she coaxed.

Cautiously, he raised his spoon to his mouth,

smelling the contents before swallowing. "Yuk!" He threw his spoon on the table and Melissa emulated his action. Starr felt her nerves snap. Jan had been gone less than an hour and she was fit to be tied.

"All right, guys, if you don't want to eat a good breakfast, I don't care."

Happy with her announcement, they hopped away from the table and settled on the couch in front of the television set.

"Oh, no you don't," Starr informed them as she returned from the kitchen after cleaning up the messy table. "We're not going to sit in front of the idiot box all day."

They both eyed her as if she were some sort of an ogre as she snapped off the set.

"What're we gonna do?" Frank asked sullenly, his bottom lip dropping into a pout. "Mommy always lets us watch TV on Sunday."

"As soon as you get dressed," Starr informed him, "we're going on a picnic."

It took her longer than she thought to get them both into shorts and cotton shirts. Finally, she perched Melissa on the front seat beside her and Frank in the back with the picnic basket, after repeatedly warning him about leaving the lid closed.

"Where're we going?" Frank asked as he kicked the seat with his sneakers.

"Frank, knock it off," Starr warned him. "You're making my headache worse."

Once she was on the highway, Frank calmed down. Breathing a sigh of relief, Starr watched the rolling hills speed by. It wouldn't be long before they would be clothed in brilliant shades of gold and crimson. The air would grow crisp, and gray tendrils of smoke would wind upward into the autumn sky. Fall was her favorite season. When autumn came, she couldn't wait to get up in the mornings, rush outside, and see what new array of blazing colors God had created while she slept. She loved the land with a deep and abiding passion, treasuring it, trying to preserve it. How hard it was to explain that love to someone like Trevor Hall, who failed to see its link with the Almighty. How sad to look at God's handiwork and see only dollar signs.

When they reached the Braden property, Starr parked the car in the same spot she had earlier in the week. She gave the blanket to Frank to carry as she grabbed Melissa with one hand and hoisted the large basket in the other. With a mischievous twinkle in her blue eyes, she lifted Melissa and Frank one at a time over the barbed-wire fence. After the picnic basket was safely on the other side, she crawled through the fence and looked around with a pleased smile.

"So much for your 'No Trespassing' sign, Mr. High and Mighty. This is West Virginia land and I'm going to enjoy it before it's gobbled up by your progress," she muttered to herself.

Although it was only midmorning, the heat of the sun grew more intense with each passing moment. Today was going to be another scorcher.

She spread the blanket under her favorite old oak and placed the basket in the shade. Frank and Melissa were running through the meadow squealing with delight in their unexpected freedom. It was difficult for Jan ever to have time to do things with them. Working six days a week at the real estate office left her precious little time for anything else. And Mrs. Ludlow, the baby-sitter, was too old to romp with them. Starr thought both of the children were far too pale and definitely spent too many hours in front of the television set.

Leaning against the rough-textured bark, she opened the pocket-sized edition of the New Testament she always carried in her purse. She read for a few minutes and then closed her eyes in the warm lull of the sun's rays. In the distance she could hear the children playing and she winced occasionally as they shrieked in excitement. Vaguely aware of the myriad summer sounds drifting through her subconscious, she pushed her hat down over her face and dozed in contentment.

"Still can't read, I see."

Slowly, Starr removed her hat and gazed up into the amused eyes. "Are you going to throw me off your property?" she asked as her blue eyes widened in mock innocence. She bestowed her most saccharine smile on him.

He laughed and sank down on the blanket across from her.

She eyed his soft pastel shirt that was unbuttoned to his waist.

"Can't stand the heat, Mr. Hall?"

"As a matter of fact, Miss Monroe, I was surveying the property and became very warm.

Out of politeness I covered myself when I saw—" He stopped in midsentence as Frank and Melissa approached them. Melissa crawled onto Starr's lap as Frank eyed Trevor with distrust. Trevor watched Starr wipe Melissa's hands with a moistened tissue.

"I told you," he said softly, "I can see you with a houseful of kids."

"If you knew the kind of morning I had, you wouldn't say that. Anyway, they're not mine. I'm not married. Remember?" She pushed her heavy dark hair back from her neck.

"I didn't think that mattered anymore," he teased as he lifted an eyebrow in amusement.

"It does here. And it would matter very much to me."

Trevor looked at Melissa's red curls. "She looks like the redhead at the real estate office."

Starr nodded. "Jan went to Huntington to see her sister today."

"Who're you?" Frank asked suddenly, after studying Trevor in silence.

Trevor laughed and solemnly offered his hand. "I'm the guy who owns this picnic ground, young man."

"Yes, dear," Starr informed Frank. "Mr. Hall's going to bulldoze the picnic ground and build great big houses with lots of people. We won't be able to come here anymore."

Trevor's green eyes were flashing warning signals which she chose to ignore.

"Why can't we come here anymore, Aunt Starr?"

"Because there won't be any trees or meadow.

There'll just be lots of houses with 'No Trespassing' signs."

Trevor's face was flushed with irritation.

"Why don't you two go play a little bit longer and then we'll eat. All right?" She shooed them off and sat upright against the oak with a look of absolute innocence.

"What happened to 'love thy neighbor'? I thought you were a Christian. You can be vicious, lady."

"You're not my neighbor. You're my enemy." Too late, she realized her mistake as she saw his triumphant smile.

"Then you're supposed to try to love me even more," he said as he reached out and grabbed her ankle, dragging her down beside him on the blanket. His strong fingers tightened around her wrists, pinning her down. An apprehensive chill swept through Starr. What was there about Trevor Hall that frightened her?

"You know, young lady, all you need is a strong man to take you in hand. A loving husband and a few children would get rid of some of that vinegar. You need proper channeling for all that misdirected energy."

"How chauvinistic, Mr. Hall. I would have thought a modern macho like you could come up with a better solution than that." Starr glared at him, but underneath her defiance she was trembling. She hoped he couldn't hear the way her heart was pounding.

His green eyes burned into hers and fear flooded through her in huge waves. It was not a fear of physical injury but rather the awareness that he had unearthed some truths she had buried from herself. Ever since Kevin, she had been running from relationships. She had become a proponent of almost any cause to avoid one-on-one contact with men.

"Let me go," Starr pleaded, afraid she was about to burst into tears.

"Why, Miss Monroe, you're actually asking me, and in a nice way!" He tightened his grip on her wrists and lowered his head close to hers.

"The children," she protested.

"They can't see us from where they're playing."

His intense, probing gaze stripped her emotions and she closed her eyes. His lips brushed her closed lids with a feather-soft touch.

"Don't, Trevor, please," she pleaded in a breathless whisper.

"What are you so afraid of?" he asked as he touched her lips tenderly with his finger. "So you were hurt once. We've all been down that road. No one gets through life without some tribulations."

He felt her body grow rigid with defiance. "Once is enough." She struggled to escape his possessive grip. "Now let me go. It's time to feed the children."

With a thoughtful, almost preoccupied look, Trevor let her go.

Starr slowly sat up, rubbing her wrists for a moment to restore the circulation. Trevor lay on his side, his thick blond hair slightly disheveled from the soft breeze that had begun to blow. With covert scrutiny he studied her from under his lowered dark brown lashes as she removed items from the picnic basket.

"Sprouts?" he asked as his nose wrinkled slightly in distaste.

"No. I'm afraid their nutritional habits are worse than yours—but then they're only children. There's still hope. I'll have them eating right yet."

"And there's no hope for me, Starr?" His large hand touched her arm lightly, resting on the smooth, tanned firmness. She paused with a boiled egg in her hand as the heat from his fingers seemed to burn through her arm to the bone. She stared at him as their eyes locked, weighing the answer to his double entendre.

"It's hard to teach an old dog new tricks," she said as she removed his hand.

His laugh echoed through the quiet meadow, and seconds later both children came running to join them.

"Would you care to join us, Mr. Hall?" Starr asked as she spread the tablecloth.

With curiosity he watched her set out the boiled eggs, carrot and celery sticks, and wrapped sandwiches. "It depends. What's in the sandwiches?"

"Peanut butter, cream cheese, raisins, and crushed potato sticks."

She handed a sandwich to him and watched as he dubiously unwrapped it. For a long moment he looked at it and then handed it back. "I'm sure you didn't plan on an extra person for your little outing."

"Chicken," she muttered under her breath as she filled the children's plates.

"Now that sounds more like it."

She was about to lecture him on the evils of eating other species when she realized he was baiting her. The wind teased her black hair with gentle fingers and she raised her arms to push it back from her warm face. His eyes mirrored his appreciation of her natural beauty and she blushed at the open admiration in his gaze.

Frank, who had been watching them with quiet curiosity, blurted, "Why're you turning red, Aunt Starr?"

With a sharp admonishment to eat his sandwich, Starr rose and walked toward the heady smell of the meadow. The drone of the fat bumblebees in the clover comforted her. She stared across the meadow at where the green field met the azure blue, cloudless sky. She stood in the tall grass absorbing the full brunt of the hot sun on her back. She wasn't aware of Trevor standing behind her until his hands gripped her shoulders and moved upward to massage her taut neck muscles. Her body went limp as she leaned against him.

"You can't run forever," he murmured against her cheek as his arms gently encircled her.

With a sigh she pulled away from him. He was weakening her already crumbling defenses. "I'm not running," she said in quiet determination as she watched the wind make undulating waves across the sea of purple clover.

He smiled as he pulled his sunglasses from his pocket and slipped them on. "You could have fooled me."

Choking back the retort that threatened to surface, Starr brushed past him. Why try to make him understand?

He turned to watch her retreating figure, his large hands resting lightly on his lean hips.

Starr quickly gathered up the basket and crammed the uneaten food into it. When she glanced up, she noticed that Trevor was still staring out across the rolling green hills. "Probably deciding where to put his stupid saunas and tennis courts," she muttered angrily to herself.

Despite Frank's plea to crawl through the barbed-wire fence again, she made him leave with her and Melissa through the open wooden gate. Melissa had grown tired and irritable from the heat. Starr handed the basket to Frank and carried Melissa to the car. As she started the motor, she was surprised to see her hands trembling. She could still feel the heat from Trevor's long fingers on her neck and shoulders.

For a pain-filled moment she thought of Kevin. She never wanted another man to have that kind of hold on her. Why had she come back to this particular spot today? Had she been hoping Trevor would be here?

As she drove, she glanced at Melissa who had

already fallen asleep with her red head resting against the door. The heat of the small car's interior was enervating. When she glanced in the rearview mirror, she wasn't surprised to see that Frank had also fallen asleep, curled up against the picnic basket. Without a backward look at the meadow, she pulled onto the highway, eager to escape the heat—and Trevor.

When Jan returned home around ten that evening, Starr had fallen asleep in front of the television.

"How's Charlotte?" Starr asked as she stretched wearily and rose from the couch.

"She's fine. We had a nice long visit." Jan studied Starr's tired face. "A handful, aren't they?"

"Uh—active," Starr admitted as she assembled her paraphernalia.

"You're welcome to stay the night if you don't want to drive home."

"Thanks anyway," Starr said as she stifled a yawn. "It's not that far. Besides, I have to feed Clem and P.J."

Jan hugged her warmly. "Thanks for taking care of the monsters."

The night air had turned cooler and Starr drove the short distance home with the car window rolled down, letting the refreshing breeze caress her warm face. She fell into bed with bone-weary exhaustion, but not before reaching for the ancient Bible on the nightstand. Her mother had taught her early in life to read at least a chapter of the Good Book upon arising in the morning and again before retiring. No matter how tired she was, she always managed to finish that one chapter before succumbing to sleep.

She wished Jan would take Frank and Melissa to church. They needed exposure to God's Word. Even Melissa, as young as she was, would benefit from regular Sunday school classes. Jan was always too tired after her long week at the realty office, but Starr hated to see her favorite children growing up without any spiritual guidance.

As she closed her eyes and snuggled into the pillow, Trevor Hall's features flashed into her mind. A smile touched her lips as she dropped off to sleep.

The next morning she barely had time for a cup of herb tea before dashing off to open the store. A forewarning of autumn was in the early morning air, and Starr filled her lungs with deep breaths, thinking of the coming season with excitement.

Abner Greenlee was waiting in front of the store for her to open. He was in his seventies with skin as soft and unlined as a baby's. She wondered what he'd run out of over the weekend.

"Good morning, Abner. Not going to be so hot today."

He switched his plug of tobacco to the other side of his cheek. "Nope. Don't look like it."

He followed her into the store as she turned on the lights and checked the freezers.

"Want a cup of tea, Abner?" Starr called as she headed for the back room.

"Nope. Need some of those vitamins you gave me last month that helped my arthritis."

Starr turned on the burner under the teakettle and carried a bottle of alfalfa tablets to the register. Her blue eyes sparkled with delight. "I'm glad to hear they helped you, Abner. Are you still taking your C's?"

He nodded as he searched through his coverall pockets for money.

"Need anything else?"

"Guess not."

"That'll be $4.24, then." Starr waited patiently while he slowly straightened out the four crumpled dollar bills and searched through his ancient change purse for the coins. She experienced a twinge of guilt as she took the money. Maybe she should have told him the vitamins were on sale. She knew he depended entirely upon his Social Security checks.

"Good morning, Miss Monroe." A tall figure loomed in the doorway.

Starr's fingers trembled as she placed the bills in the drawer. "Good morning, Mr. Hall," she responded in a businesslike manner before returning her attention to Abner. "I've put a little sample in your sack for Ellie, Abner. Tell her to use it instead of sugar. All right?"

He nodded and muttered a gruff "Good morning" to Trevor as he left with his purchase tucked safely in his faded coveralls.

Without speaking to her again, Trevor sauntered lazily around the store, picking up bottles, sniffing at unfamiliar substances, and checking prices. In vain, Starr tried to keep her mind on the order form in front of her, but the lines kept running together. What was he doing?

Finally, he deposited himself in the old plastic chair and crossed his long legs nonchalantly. "You're a terrible businesswoman," he commented with a deep sigh of resignation. "I don't know how you've managed to stay in business as long as you have."

"Of all the nerve—" Starr sputtered.

"You didn't even want to charge that old guy for the vitamins."

Starr opened her mouth to protest but he cut her off.

"Don't deny it. I saw it in your face when you were counting out his money."

The teakettle began to whistle and she dashed for the back room. Angrily, she grabbed the pot from the burner and tossed a tea bag into the cup. "Darn, darn, darn," she muttered as the water splashed on her finger. He made her so angry she could scream. But he was right. She didn't like to take Abner's money.

She sensed rather than heard him behind her. "Would you like a cup of tea, Mr. Hall?" Even though she made a great effort to keep her voice steady, she could hear the tremor in it.

His hand closed over hers and he turned it over slowly to see what she was holding. "Is it dandelion or something equally exotic?" he teased.

42

Starr jerked her hand away from his strong fingers. "Rose hips. It's very tasty—and good for you." She couldn't help adding the last part. She handed him the cup and watched him take a tentative sip.

"Yuk," he said with a sour grimace.

"You're as bad as Jan's children." By now her sense of humor was overriding her irritation. She took his cup and added a small amount of honey. Suddenly aware of his dominating presence in the small room, she thrust the cup into his hand and hurried back into the store. He followed her, slowly sipping the tea.

"Well?" she asked, turning to face him and nearly colliding with him, unaware that he had been so close behind her. "What do you think now?"

"It's still awful, but at least now it's sweet."

Rolling her blue eyes heavenward, Starr sighed in exasperation. "Honestly, Trevor."

"That sounds better than Mr. Hall," he said softly as he placed his cup on the counter and took her in his arms.

She gazed into his serious green eyes with a stunned expression. "Please, Trevor. Someone might walk in." She pushed against his chest but his arms only tightened.

"Don't kid me, Starr. You don't have that much business on Monday mornings."

"How would you—"

He silenced her question with his warm lips. The clean, crisp smell of his after-shave permeated her senses as she responded to his tender kiss. As her slim brown arms slipped around his neck, she chastised herself. What was wrong with her? Trevor Hall was not a man to be trusted. He stood for everything she hated.

Shoving those thoughts into the deeper recesses of her mind, Starr surrendered to the warmth of his arms.

THREE
A Time
to Forget

Trevor's kiss left Starr shaken and confused. When she opened her eyes at last, his teasing expression was the first thing she saw. Was he making fun of her again? Her blue eyes flashed with a brief anger as she pulled abruptly out of his embrace.

As she withdrew from his arms, he laughed softly, the sound of it making little shivery patterns chase up and down her spine. Starr busied herself at the already tidy counter, setting out samples, doing anything to occupy her trembling fingers. Her heart pounded with a furious thudding as she struggled to regain her air of detachment. She could feel his presence behind her as he studied and analyzed her from behind those thick, lowered lashes.

"Who was he?" he asked finally.

She froze. "Who was who?" Eyes wide with surprise, she turned to face him.

"The guy who was foolish enough to let you get away."

In the narrow space behind the counter their eyes locked for a long moment before she lowered her gaze.

"It wasn't that way at all," Starr whispered, her cheeks burning with shame. "He jilted me at the last minute. At the church." Her voice had dropped so low Trevor had to strain to hear what she was saying. This time the shocked expression appeared on his face.

"You're kidding!" The exclamation burst from him as he stared at her in disbelief.

"No," she admitted as the memory of that horrible day returned full force. "I'm not kidding."

"But why?" Trevor couldn't seem to comprehend what she was telling him.

Unable to answer, she turned away as the lump welled up in her constricted throat.

"Starr?" His hands were warm on her shoulders. She could feel the strength of his lean fingers.

"I don't want to discuss my personal life with a—a complete stranger." Shocked at how much of her private life she had already divulged in a moment of weakness, she turned defensive again to cover her fear. Her blue eyes were dark with unspoken pain.

Trevor dropped his hands and moved from behind the counter. "At least you didn't say perfect stranger."

46

Starr gave a faint smile for his weak attempt at humor.

At the shop door he hesitated as a thoughtful look flickered in his intense eyes. "You threatened him. You knew that, didn't you? He was afraid of you." He continued to study her tall figure for a long, pensive moment. "A lot of men would be terrified of you, Starr Monroe. You're much too strong for most men."

Fighting to hold back the pent-up tears, she kept her head down. When at last she looked up, he was gone.

Starr gazed at the empty space for a long time. Life went on. Summer days always turned to fall and winter eventually came. Spring. Summer. Fall. Winter. There was a season for everything.

She softly recited the words from Ecclesiastes that had brought her so much comfort through the years:

> To every thing there is a season, and a time to every purpose under the heaven:
> A time to be born, and a time to die; a time to plant, and a time to pluck up that which is planted;
> A time to kill, and a time to heal; a time to break down, and a time to build up;
> A time to weep, and a time to laugh; a time to mourn, and a time to dance;
> A time to cast away stones, and a time to gather stones together; a time to embrace, and a time to refrain from embracing;
> A time to get, and a time to lose; a time to keep, and a time to cast away;

A time to rend, and a time to sew; a time to
    keep silence, and a time to speak;
A time to love, and a time to hate; a time of
    war, and a time of peace.

The words still echoed in her mind as she
thought of that August day when she had stood
at the altar waiting for a bridegroom who never
came. She had never seen him again. There had
been a brief note saying he was sorry. Sorry. Her
whole life had fallen apart and he was sorry. She
knew people in Springfield still felt sorry for her,
whispered about what had happened. Tears
washed down her cheeks. Jilted. Left at the altar
on what should have been the happiest day of
her life.

The credo "Once burned, twice shy" had
guided her life from that day forward. Slowly,
one by one, any would-be suitors had faded
away. Although no one mentioned the catastro-
phe anymore, Starr always felt its ghost lingering in the backs of their minds. Whenever she
entered a room and the conversation suddenly
stopped, she wondered if her ill-fated romance
had been the topic. After Kevin's abrupt departure from Springfield, she had thrown herself
more and more into church and civic affairs.
Whether to hide the bitterness or to ease the
ever-present hurt, she didn't know. Only Jan
dared to approach directly the forbidden subject, telling her repeatedly she shouldn't let her
experience with Kevin prejudice her entire opinion of the male gender. Starr turned deaf ears to
Jan's advice and discouraged her matchmaking

attempts with the same obstinate refusals. Surprisingly, their friendship not only survived but grew stronger. Since Frank's death, Starr had been the one who offered solace most often.

Starr was still lost in thoughts of the past when Jan came in a little before noon.

"Hi. How about going out for a real meal for a change? I'm sick of sandwiches. The café has tuna casserole today." Her brown eyes glowed with an enthusiasm that even the heat couldn't dim.

"Well," Starr commented, glancing around the deserted store, "why not? I don't think I'm going to miss too many customers."

The heat was stifling as they slowly walked down Main Street to the café. Once inside the cool restaurant, they found an empty booth toward the back and sank gratefully into the well-worn red leather seats.

"Have you seen your boyfriend since he was in the other day?"

Starr choked on a piece of ice. "What? Who're you talking about?" The flush on her cheeks belied her innocent expression.

"I mean the only tall, good-looking man you've met lately — Trevor Hall."

"Oh, him," Starr muttered as she studied the shabby menu with feigned concentration.

"I don't know why you're even looking at that menu, Starr. You know the only thing you'll eat is the tuna. I think you're avoiding my question."

Sighing in defeat, Starr closed the menu and slid it behind the napkin holder. "Yes, I saw him again and he was nice enough to tell me what a lousy businesswoman I am. He sure has some nerve. I'll say that for him." Anger spread anew as she thought about his comments. She omitted telling Jan about the kiss. Her mouth still tingled from the memory of it. He was the most audacious man.

"Oh, I don't know, Starr," Jan said with a sly smile. "I think he's pretty nice."

Starr gave a derisive snort. She was saved from commenting further when Millie approached to take their orders.

They were halfway through their luncheon when a voice that was growing increasingly familiar greeted them.

"Why, hello, Mrs. Stevens, Miss Monroe."

Starr, reluctantly raising her gaze from her plate, met Trevor's laughing green eyes. A shorter man with a full, silky brown beard was with him.

At that moment Starr swallowed a piece of the casserole the wrong way and began to cough until her eyes were watering.

As Trevor advanced toward her, she shrank back against the booth.

"I'm well versed in the Heimlich method, Miss Monroe," he assured her as she shook her head violently in protest.

"Don't you dare," she managed to gasp between fits of coughing.

As Trevor slid into the booth beside her, he bestowed a dazzling smile on her. "The place is full. Do you two mind if we join you?"

Before Starr could refuse, Jan spoke up. "We'd be delighted, Mr. Hall."

"Trevor, please," he admonished her with another charming smile.

The bearded man seated himself by Jan after giving her a shy smile.

Starr continued to cough, pressing her napkin to her lips. Trevor glanced at her in amusement and tasted her casserole.

"Seems harmless enough. I think I'll have the tuna also," he told Millie, who was watching the whole scene with wide-eyed delight.

When they had ordered, Trevor smiled at Jan.

"Ladies, this is my construction foreman, Bob Mason. Bob, this is Mrs. Stevens who works in the real estate office down the street, and this," he turned to a still red-faced Starr, "is Miss Starr Monroe, local entrepreneur, nutritionist, and general do-gooder."

His emphasis on her single state for the second time infuriated her and she shot daggers at him. She was surprised to see Trevor was dressed in a well-worn work shirt and faded denim jeans.

Bob nodded and smiled pleasantly at Starr before turning his undivided attention to Jan.

"Trevor says you're a widow." His dark eyes were filled with warmth and compassion.

Half-listening to the conversation, Starr stared at the remainder of her casserole, unable to eat another bite. Furious at Trevor for interrupting her meal with Jan, she kept her eyes on her uneaten lunch. She could feel his eyes on her and her cheeks grew warm under his examination.

"Aren't you going to finish your lunch?" he asked with an innocent smile.

Starr gave him a withering glare. "I seem to have lost my appetite."

"That's a shame," he commented as he reached to remove her plate.

Starr watched in utter amazement as he finished her lunch without the slightest comment. Much to her discomfort, Jan and Bob were watching the two of them in thinly veiled amusement.

"Do you always clean up other people's plates?" she hissed under her breath.

"No, but you weren't going to eat it. And I know how ecology-minded you are. 'Waste not, want not,'" he quoted cheerfully as her cheeks flamed with repressed anger.

Caught for once without a retort, Starr glared at Jan for inviting him to join them. But Jan looked away to smile at Bob Mason, leaving Starr to cope with Trevor as best she could.

Out of the corner of her eye she watched his dark fingers toy with the water glass. After she failed to respond to his barb, he had fallen silent. She wished Jan would hurry up with her meat loaf so they could leave. She didn't want to remain while Trevor tormented her throughout his lunch. Her last meal with him had been anything but pleasant. How she had ever let herself respond to his kisses was beyond her imagination. Very much aware of his inquisitive green eyes, she tried to maintain an icy composure.

"How was business this morning?"

She beamed a frigid glance in his direction. "Wonderful," she said, with no attempt to hide her sarcasm. "I had to hand out numbers to handle the rush."

"You know if you—" he began as she rose angrily from the booth. Another lecture from him on how to run her business she didn't need. Starr grabbed her purse and knocked over her water, dumping the contents into Trevor's lap.

As the cold water drenched his jeans, he jumped to his feet in shock, upsetting his own water, which further deluged his legs.

As he tried to mop the wetness from his pants, Starr took advantage of his preoccupation and ran from the café. She fled down Main Street until she reached the sanctuary of her shop. She left the "Out to Lunch" sign on the closed door, fearful he would follow her in retaliation.

In the back room of the shop she tried to suppress the smile that quivered on her lips as she thought of him finishing his lunch, drenched to the skin. The laughter started as a tiny spiral that wound higher and higher until she was holding her sides in agony. It had been an accident, she assured herself, but it had been lovely indeed to see that superior smirk wiped from his handsome face for once. She finally managed to get herself under control and unlock the shop for business.

The afternoon passed slowly, as only about a half-dozen of her faithful customers purchased a few vitamins and toiletries. She was engrossed in the latest issue of **Prevention** magazine when she heard the bell chime. She looked up and recognized Bob Mason almost immediately.

He stood awkwardly at the door, looking around the small store. He cleared his throat and approached her as she silently watched him, wondering if Trevor had sent him for some reason.

"I wonder if you could help me, Miss Monroe," he ventured softly.

She shut the magazine carefully. "Did Trevor Hall send you here?" she asked in a deliberately direct manner.

"Well, no," he said, rather startled at her question. "You see, I just got into town yesterday and it seems I'm allergic to something at the construction site."

Now that he was closer, Starr noticed his puffy eyes, which were tearing. His nose seemed awfully red, and not from a sunburn, either.

"Hay fever," she said as he coughed slightly.

"Hay fever!" he echoed incredulously. "I've never had hay fever that I can remember."

"Well, you're suffering from it now," she informed him as she reached for the vitamin C capsules. "Take these three times a day: morning, noon, and night. It wouldn't hurt either if you drank a cup of comfrey tea sweetened with honey in the morning before breakfast and again in the evening. Also, you need to take at least fifty milligrams of pantothenic acid daily."

"Sure," Bob agreed as he took out his billfold. "I'll give anything a try. You seem to know what you're talking about."

54

She rang up his purchases and put them in a small bag.

After he paid, he continued to look around the store with nervous little glances at the shelves and at Starr.

A sudden flash of comprehension dawned on Starr. "Are you sure Trevor didn't tell you to come here?" She certainly didn't need him feeling sorry for her because business was slow.

"No," he said with an embarrassed grin. "In fact, it was Jan who said you'd probably know what was in those weeds where we're working that was bothering me. Trevor wanted me to go to the doctor."

A startled look appeared in Starr's wide blue eyes. Jan? Already he was on a first-name basis.

"Oh," she replied with a cool smile that hid an inner rage. Of course Trevor would send his foreman to the doctor instead of to the local health food nut.

Bob sat down in the rickety plastic chair. "I confess I came by also because I wanted to talk to you about Jan."

Starr leaned on the counter, resting her tanned face in her hands as she watched him warily. "What about Jan?" She realized she wasn't making the conversation easy for him and he did seem like such a nice person. But an inner anger still boiled somewhere deep inside at Trevor and his high-handed attitudes.

"She seems like such a lovely lady," Bob blurted in embarrassment.

Starr stared at him in amazement. He liked Jan! He was asking questions because he was interested in her! Warming to him at last, she seated herself by him in the other plastic chair.

"She is a lovely person—inside and out."

Bob traced the fold in the paper bag with his large, work-worn hands. "How long has she been a widow?"

"Two years. And it hasn't been easy. She doesn't have any family here. Only a sister in Huntington."

"Do you think she'd go out with me?" he asked in a breathless rush.

His question caught her by surprise. "I—I don't know," Starr stammered. "I don't think Jan has dated anyone since Frank was killed."

"I see." Crestfallen, he started to rise from the chair.

"You could ask," Starr pointed out in a gentle rebuke. "She won't bite."

He laughed. "I just don't want to come on too strong. After all, I only met her, and she doesn't know anything about me."

"I'll be seeing her tonight. I have to stop there on my way home. I'll see how she feels about going out with you."

He looked uncomfortable.

"I'll be subtle," Starr assured him with a warm laugh.

From the shop window she watched Bob strolling down Main Street, looking in the windows. What a nice man he is, she thought as he stopped to talk to a couple of children who were coming out of the drugstore. How can such a sweet man work for an egotistical, overbearing person like Trevor Hall?

A little after five, Starr emptied the cash register and closed the store. She could make her deposit on the way to work in the morning. Not that it was enough to worry about anyway.

Before she reached the Braden place, she could hear the bulldozers. From her vantage point on Turkey Knob she watched the big yellow machines chewing up the green meadow in great chunks. Horror-stricken, she saw a huge oak fall with a deafening thud in the late afternoon sun. A sick feeling of loss and devastation wrenched her heart. A cloud of dust swirled around the huge earthmovers as they tenaciously dug into the virgin soil, uprooting everything in their paths. The drone of the big motors drowned out the normally serene sounds of nature and filled the warm evening air with a horrible, unnatural buzzing.

Trevor certainly wasn't wasting any time getting started. August seemed awfully late in the season to be breaking ground, she mused as she peered through her sunglasses at the melee of activity. Maybe Trevor didn't realize he wouldn't be able to build all year in West Virginia. But such an astute businessman would surely have considered that. Starr realized with a disquieting pang that she had been subconsciously looking for his familiar blond mane.

For a few more agonizing minutes Starr watched the destruction of the once peaceful meadow through her car window. Anger lodged in her chest as she drove down the road, still able to hear the muffled sound of the big motors long after she had left.

FOUR
Council
Meeting

Starr winced, thinking of the headache that
would follow the meeting, as Mayor Russell lit
his large cigar. She glanced around at the other
members who made up the Springfield City
Council. Although she was the only woman in
the group, she didn't feel out of place. Her male
constituents had been surprised when she was
elected to the council, but had welcomed her
after recovering from their shock . . . perhaps not
all with the same degree of enthusiasm. But
eventually even John Evers, who thought women
belonged only in the kitchen, thawed when he
realized how seriously she took her office. They
had since served on several committees, and his
antiquated concepts about women's roles in
society had gradually changed. Last Christmas
he had given her a T-shirt with the logo: "A
woman's place is in the house." And on the back
of the shirt was printed: "And in the Senate."

Mayor Russell had been a good friend of her father's and had delivered the eulogy at his funeral. For that reason, Starr continued to find it difficult to confront him openly about his atrocious cigar smoking. She could hear her dad saying, "Be tolerant, Starr. Don't be so quick to complain or judge."

Suffering in silence every Wednesday as the mayor puffed on in blissful ignorance, Starr often thought about leaving antismoking material at his honor's seat, but was afraid he'd know who had done it.

As she drove home from those weekly meetings with red, puffy eyes, she would say to her departed father, "Satisfied, Dad?"

Burton had complained on numerous occasions, but to no avail. Since the two of them were the only ones on the council who didn't smoke, they conceded defeat but continued to open every window in the room, regardless of the weather.

Starr looked up as Burton Ellis caught her eye and pinched his nose with his thumb and index finger, all the while looking at the mayor's offensive cigar. Starr nodded in agreement. Since the meeting had not yet officially begun, Starr slipped to the window in what she hoped was an unobtrusive manner, and opened it as far as it would go.

Burton followed her.

"Trying to get that final breath of good air?" he teased as he stood beside her, resting his hand on hers.

She smiled and moved slightly away from him on the pretext of rearranging the shade. Burton was an extremely good-looking man in his middle thirties who was well known for his roving eye. His dark hair was sprinkled with the first touches of gray. His constant flirting irritated rather than complimented Starr. Staring at him for a moment, Starr wondered if he would ever grow up.

"Burt, you and Starr ready to start the meeting?"

Glad of the mayor's interruption, Starr hurried to her seat.

As the mayor called the meeting to order, she gazed from under her lashes at Burton. Maybe she was too critical, as her dad had often pointed out to her. But Burt's constant come-ons were downright annoying and embarrassing at times. He had even made overtures to Jan shortly after Frank had died. Starr glanced away from him. He was winking at her again. He never gives up, she thought as she turned her attention to what Mayor Russell was saying. They voted on some routine issues, and Starr was leaning back in the swivel chair when she heard Trevor Hall's name mentioned. Immediately, she came to life and sat upright, her blue eyes aglow with interest.

"As you know," the mayor began, "the Springfield City Council has long been noted for taking a cautious approach to growth in our area. The council has also taken aggressive control of land-use decisions. Nor have we been too responsive to out-of-state developers. A week ago we issued a temporary building permit to Hall Development of Orange, California, for the tentative construction of a new housing development on Pat Braden's old property."

Starr frowned. She had missed last week's meeting because of an out-of-town trip with her Youth For Christ group.

"I need your support on this proposal. In the past our council has shown a great reluctance to approve any new construction by outside firms. Neither have we approved time extensions, which has caused a great deal of financial hardship for some of our larger developers. I realize we must be careful about approving vacant land development because poor planning will endanger our fair city's future. But I urge you to listen closely to Mr. Hall's proposal and give him the necessary approval that will eventually benefit us all."

Mayor Russell cleared his throat. "Mr. Hall has graciously consented to come here tonight and discuss the project that his company is developing on the Braden property. Judy, tell Mr. Hall we're ready for him now."

Hopes to develop, Starr thought as Trevor strode into the small room. He's already begun. Tall and dynamic in a soft blue summer suit, Trevor's blond hair glistened in the lights. As he glanced around the room, a look of incredulity touched his eyes when his gaze fell on Starr.

Mayor Russell took his seat, leaving the floor to Trevor, who smiled at the six council members in his most charming manner. Starr gazed back at him with a blank, noncommittal look. *What does he want now? He already has his temporary permit to begin his eyesore.* Despite her earlier pleas, he obviously intended to pursue his aim full-speed ahead. *Well,* she thought, resting her chin in her hand, *he can plead until he is blue in the face, but he isn't getting my vote.*

"Mayor Russell, members of the council, I'm sure most of you know by now that my company has purchased the Braden property east of town. Among other things, we're planning on building individual homes and a few condominiums on that tract. I'm sure some of you are wondering why we chose this particular area of the country in which to build our development." He smiled, and everyone in the room except Starr returned his smile. She sat granite-faced, waiting for his explanation.

"This is a strategically located state—as it is within a five-hundred-mile radius of more than half the population of the country. It is also an energy-rich state with an abundance of water and coal for industrial and commercial use."

"Why didn't you build in California?" Starr asked as the mayor looked at her in surprise.

"A good question, Miss Monroe. Land is at an all-time premium in California. A great deal of this project is experimental." He looked around the room at the curious expressions.

"I met Mr. Braden last year while he was visiting his daughter and son-in-law in California. We discussed my project and the prohibitive cost of land in California. He encouraged me to investigate the possibilities of moving my plans to this area and applying for a government grant to help finance it. From his description of the property I knew it was perfect for what I wanted. After Pat Braden's death, his wife had no desire to retain the property, so I purchased it immediately. I had already flown out here as Pat's guest and looked over the property carefully. It was exactly what I had in mind."

"How lucky for us," Starr said with dry sarcasm.

Undaunted by her remark, Trevor continued. "As the state government is willing to underwrite a great portion of the cost, I think it may well be a great opportunity for us all. Springfield will stand to reap sizable financial benefits if my ideas work."

"What kind of ideas?" Burton asked as he cast a critical eye at Trevor's mane of blond hair. "You going to have some kind of hippie communes like you do in California?"

Trevor laughed politely. "No, let me assure you that's the farthest thing from my mind. What I'm hoping to accomplish in this project is a low-cost housing plan that will incorporate solar heating with your own low energy costs to provide an alternative to the current offerings available. This housing would be offered to all qualified local people. We feel we can offer a better quality housing than could be found in Huntington or any other city of comparable size. As you know, this will offer employment for a great many local workers who I understand have been out of work for a few months."

The mayor was nodding in approval with a large, happy smile covering his round face. He chomped his cigar with unconcealed enthusiasm.

Trevor glanced at each of the council members as he concluded his speech. "I have some other plans, but I'd rather not reveal the details at this time. I do know this development will bring some much-needed employment into the area, and I don't think anyone's going to complain about that. I ask for your support to continue." He flashed a winning smile and sat down.

There was a general murmur of assent among the members. It would reflect well on the mayor and the council if jobs were made available to the community because of their approval of the plan.

Starr felt a slow rise of anger burning in her chest. If she voted against the project, she suspected hers would be the only dissenting vote cast. As she looked around at the enthusiastic expressions, she realized any hope of a three-member block was impossible.

The discussion was thrown open and was tossed about for nearly an hour. Starr remained silent, listening to what her fellow members were saying. She was biased and didn't want to be guilty of carrying her personal prejudices into her business life. Although she had voted against every project of this nature since gaining her council seat, she was willing to listen to what her fellow members thought about Trevor's development.

"I think," Mayor Russell was saying, "we

should all agree to give Mr. Hall and his fine company as much help as we can. After all, this will mean jobs and income for the local merchants." He gave the council members a hard, appraising stare. Most of them were local business people who would stand to gain from an influx of people into the area.

"How many men will you be hiring, Mr. Hall?" Sal Goldman asked.

"We eventually hope to employ over a hundred local people," Trevor explained. "I'll have some of my own men coming in from California to do some specialty work. I've been in contact with several engineers who are eager to try some new concepts that this project entails."

Starr watched Trevor in suspicion. What new ideas was he talking about? Was it just a line to get in good with the council? Obviously he already had the mayor eating out of his hand. She noticed that even Burton was patting him on the back, treating him like an old friend.

Since the temporary permit had already been extended, Sal asked that the final vote be delayed until the next meeting. The motion was carried unanimously.

As soon as the meeting was officially dismissed, Starr slipped out of the smoky room. She wasn't sure how much longer she could stand watching Trevor spread that million-dollar charm.

The cool night air was a pleasant shock on her flushed face as she left the courthouse and walked down the deserted main street of town. Lifting her long black hair, she let the breeze cool the thin layer of perspiration on her neck.

She stopped beside her car and kicked the low tire in frustration.

"Ouch," she muttered as the pain shot up her leg.

"I bet your foot gives out before the tire," an amused voice commented from the shadows.

Startled, she whirled around to face Trevor. Her blue eyes sparkled like brilliant diamonds under the street light.

"My goodness, how did you escape from your adoring public?"

"The same way you did. I doubt if they know I'm gone."

"Oh, I'm sure your departure was noticed." Her voice was dripping with open sarcasm.

He caught her wrist with a vicelike grip and pulled her close to him. His green eyes taunted her as her heart pounded wildly.

"Let me go, you arrogant, spoiled—"

"When you run out of complimentary adjectives, let me know." His breath was warm against her cheek, creating a delicious tingle down the side of her body. Confused, she stopped struggling as his lips touched hers gently, but with a masterful command. Her long arms circled his neck hesitantly at first and then tightened as she returned his kiss. The gentle scratch of his beard tickled her cheek as he seemed to envelope her, his arms crushing her to him in an age-old gesture of dominance. She surrendered with only a half-hearted attempt at resistance. Time became a nebulous entity as she clung to him, lost in the magic of the moment.

When at last the kiss ended, Trevor still held her, tightly locked in his embrace. "Now that's a lot better than when you fight." He grinned, looking down at her flushed cheeks.

Starr's eyes flashed as she stiffened in his arms.

"Have I violated some great feminist principle? I like for a woman to enjoy being kissed by me."

"I'm sure there are many who will testify to that rather dubious pleasure. Now, let me go. I have to get home. I have reports to read." With a determined jerk, she broke free of his embrace.

Trevor watched in amusement as she strode around to the driver's side of the car.

"Too bad you didn't stay for lunch the other day," he called as she urged the motor to life.

Starr rolled down the window and glared at him for a final time. "Why? Did you clean all the plates?" With a squeal of tires she shot down Main Street and away from his disturbing presence.

Trevor continued to gaze down the deserted street for a few moments before returning to the courthouse.

Starr drove the short distance from the courthouse to the diner at a reckless speed. When she parked in front of the diner, she pulled the emergency brake with such force that she wouldn't have been surprised to find it detached and hanging useless in her shaking hand. Trevor seemed to appear at every unlikely place—and when she least expected him. She hurried to the back of the diner and seated herself in a small booth next to the kitchen. Her breath was still coming in ragged gasps and she wasn't sure she could trust herself to hold a conversation with anyone. When Millie appeared with pad in hand, she ordered a small salad and cup of tea.

She was congratulating herself on the restoration of her emotional stability when she became aware of someone standing by the booth. Oh, no, she groaned inwardly as she raised her head from reading the minutes of the previous week's council meeting. Relief flooded through her when she saw Laura Ames and Alison McGee from the youth group at church.

"Hi, Starr," they greeted her.

Starr folded the council minutes and slid them beneath her purse. "Hi, girls. What's up?"

They exchanged nervous glances.

"We don't want to bother you," Laura began hesitantly.

"Sit," Starr said as she moved over to make room for them. It was apparent that something was bothering them. And problems were just as big at sixteen as they were at sixty.

Both girls slid into the small booth just as Millie arrived with Starr's salad.

"Would you girls like something to eat?"

"No," Alison said, "but I wouldn't mind a Coke."

"Same with me," added Laura.

Too tired to give a nutritional lecture, Starr waited until their soft drinks arrived before starting on her salad.

"What's the problem, ladies?" she inquired as she sipped her tea.

"It's sort of a big problem," Laura murmured as she twisted the straw wrapper, avoiding Starr's probing blue eyes.

Starr glanced at Alison, who also quickly looked away. Maybe it was a bigger problem than she had thought. Starr continued eating her salad as she waited for them to broach the subject that was bothering them.

Finally Laura blurted, "We have this friend who's in trouble."

Starr felt the lettuce stick in her throat as she glanced from Laura's lovely heart-shaped face to Alison's freckles. A horrible suspicion crossed her mind and they read the thought in her eyes.

"It's not us, Starr. Honest," they chorused in unison.

"Oh." Starr pushed the rest of her salad aside and studied both girls with an unwavering appraisal. "What kind of trouble is your friend in?"

"Her boyfriend wants her to quit school and get married," Alison volunteered.

"And her parents will kill her if she does," Laura finished.

A soft sigh escaped from Starr. Of course, they had to be talking about Mary Lou Williams, who had been dating Don Hoover. At twenty-two, Don was much too mature for Mary Lou. No wonder her folks were having such a fit.

Both Alison and Laura were watching her, waiting for her advice.

"Your friend is only sixteen, isn't she?" Starr asked as they nodded in answer. "And her parents would be very upset if she married at her age?"

"Her parents don't really love her," Alison blurted.

Starr chose her words with careful precision. She had worked so hard to gain the confidence of her youth group. If she wasn't careful, she was going to blow it all within the next five minutes.

"You mean because they don't approve of her dating someone who's six years older?"

Laura and Alison exchanged quick glances. "We didn't say how old her boyfriend is," Laura said.

"I know," Starr explained in a gentle tone. "I've known for some time that Mary Lou has been seeing Don instead of coming to church for the youth meetings."

Both girls fell silent as they realized that Starr was aware of their friend's secret.

"You feel her folks are unreasonable, don't you? You think at sixteen Mary Lou should be able to decide what she wants."

"Well, yes," Laura concurred as her soft brown eyes blazed with the strength of her convictions. "They love each other. Why shouldn't they get married?"

"Because she's only sixteen, and although Don is six years older, at their ages it makes a big difference. Mary Lou should at least finish high school before thinking of marriage."

One look at their stony faces and Starr sensed she had alienated them.

"We thought you'd understand," Alison said

as she pushed her Coke away. "We could always talk to you, Starr. It's not like trying to talk to our parents. They never listen anyway."

Again, Starr chose her words with the precision of a dentist's drill. "Your parents love you so very much, it's hard for them to remain emotionally uninvolved when you're having problems. They really want only the best for you, as I'm sure Mary Lou's folks want only the best for her."

Alison continued to stare at the table as Laura nodded with an unconvinced look in her big brown eyes.

"Why don't you tell Mary Lou to come and talk to me? Tell her to stop by the store after school some afternoon."

"She'll know we told," Alison said with a despondent shrug.

"No. I won't give you away. Just say I want to see her. I won't say anything about our little talk."

"Oh, Starr, that would be wonderful," Laura gushed as her face lit up with a happy smile. "Mary Lou will listen to you."

After the girls had left, Starr sat staring into space with a thoughtful expression. How strange that she should be advising someone else on the pitfalls of marriage.

As she gathered her unread report and her purse, she thought that God really did move in mysterious ways.

FIVE
Sunday
Dinner

Starr didn't see Trevor again until the Sunday morning following the council meeting. Tired as she was from the frustrations of the week and the heat, she didn't want to miss church again.

As she hurried from the parking lot up the front steps, the organist was playing "Church in the Wildwood." The morning sun bathed the white frame church in a golden glow as the stained-glass windows sparkled in a kaleidoscope of colors. A lightness touched her heart and Starr eagerly ran up the steps.

Every seat was taken. She looked around in dismay. Slowly, she made her way down front, looking on each side of the aisle for a vacancy. Had she known it was going to be this crowded.... Her eyes sparkled. She had spotted an empty seat on the end. Not until she had arranged her purse and picked up the hymnal did she glance at her companion.

"Good morning, Miss Monroe. What a pleasant surprise to see you here. I thought you'd be resting on your day off."

Just inches away from her astonished gaze were Trevor Hall's mocking green eyes.

"What are you doing here?" she whispered as she opened the hymnbook.

"Why, Miss Monroe, the same as you—looking for a little spiritual fulfillment and guidance."

Starr smoothed her light blue skirt and folded her hands in her lap when she saw that he was looking at them. Suddenly, she was conscious of their plainness. Because she used her hands for practical purposes, she kept her nails short and unpolished. She grew uncomfortably warm as she stared straight ahead at the altar.

"Are you sure you haven't wandered into the wrong building?" she asked as she glanced at his blond profile from the corner of her eye.

"Naughty," he answered with a raise of his eyebrow. "You have such a suspicious mind, Starr. Don't you trust anyone?"

"I bet you don't go to church in California."

Crossing his leg, he moved closer to her as she edged toward the aisle. "Watch out or you'll be sitting on the floor in a most embarrassing heap," Trevor warned. "And you lose your bet. I go to church—every Sunday. Except last week. I had to survey some property. Remember?"

Starr grabbed his arm to keep from falling off the end of the pew. "Oh, I forgot," she murmured, letting go of his arm as though he had a contagious disease, "it's a good place to be seen."

His soft laughter filled her ears. "My dear Miss Monroe, your heart is harder than the Pharaoh's."

"Oh, you—"

At that moment Reverend Hartford stepped to the pulpit and Starr choked back her retort, aware that Trevor was still watching her with an amused smile.

She sighed inwardly as Reverend Hartford announced the topic of his sermon: Love Thy Neighbor. She didn't trust herself to look over at Trevor.

"Of all the commandments that Jesus gave us, one of the most important ones is to love our neighbor. Only loving God with all our hearts is more important. If you practice these two commandments, the rest of your life will fall into perfect order. Divine order. Love God. Love your fellowman."

Reverend Hartford's blue eyes sparkled with animation as he continued. "How simple it sounds, and yet how hard it is for most of us to put these two simple laws into practice. Yes," he declared, pounding his palm with his fist, "it means loving that crabby next-door neighbor who lets her dog dig up your flowers. Yes, it means loving that person who makes fun of you, belittles you, hurts you. Yes, it means loving your mother-in-law."

A few nervous titters of guilt met that statement. Starr felt her anxieties fading as she tuned in to the reverend.

"Love. One little word composed of four letters. Yet it is by far the most powerful word in the world. Love can work miracles. Heal broken hearts. Love. Love your neighbor as much as you love yourself. Love your enemy and you will confront him with a weapon far more powerful than a nuclear bomb. LOVE!" Reverend Hartford thundered as he raised his arms heavenward.

Starr trembled from the power of his words. How simple it was in theory, but how hard to apply in everyday life. As they stood to sing the closing hymn, she was surprised to hear Trevor's lovely baritone voice. She was even more surprised that he knew the words without looking at the hymnal.

As soon as the final blessing was given, she turned on her heel and hurried down the church aisle. Trevor Hall was much too disturbing a man to be constantly at odds with him. For a horrible moment she wondered if he planned these incidents. She wouldn't put it past him. He had more nerve than any man she'd ever met. Except Kevin, that is.

A hand closed over hers as she started to open the car door. She didn't bother to look up.

"Yes, Mr. Hall, what is it now?" She didn't try to keep the irritation from her voice.

"I believe you owe me a dinner," he said with that innocent smile lighting his face.

"What?" Exasperated, Starr stood facing him, hands on her hips as the wind teased her black hair with gentle tugs. "I owe you a dinner?" she squeaked.

"That's right," he insisted as he moved closer to her, smiling down into the sea-blue eyes that were agog with sheer disbelief.

She popped her sunglasses over her eyes. "You're crazy. I believe you collected for that dinner." A flush crept up her neck the minute those ill-chosen words left her lips. She vividly recalled the kiss he had collected as clearly as anything that had ever happened in her entire life.

Trevor tilted her chin. "Not in full," he assured her in a husky voice. For an electrifying moment she thought he was going to kiss her in the church parking lot.

"What do you want?" she repeated in a quarrelsome tone. "Do you want me to buy you a dinner? Why don't I just give you a check and you can go eat by yourself? I have chores to finish. This is my only day off and I don't intend to stand here arguing with you about your stomach!"

"Good." He strode around to the other side of her car and let himself in. "Let's go home, then."

Shaking with disbelief, Starr slid behind the wheel and started the motor. The church lot was rapidly filling and several people waved at Starr. She forced herself to smile and wave.

With the smile still frozen on her lips, she turned to him. "You're impossible. You know that, don't you?" she flung at him as they turned onto the highway

When he didn't answer, she looked closer at

him. His eyes were closed and the sun bathed his tanned face in a soft glow, highlighting the blond gleam of his full, long hair.

"You wear your hair too long," she said gruffly to hide the strange sensation that crept slowly across her chest.

He turned his head sideways on the bucket seat and smiled at her with a lazy lift of his eyelids. "You're the first gal who ever complained about my hair. Do you want me to cut it?"

Starr quickly jerked her eyes back to the winding highway. "I'm not a gal and I don't care what you do with your hair," she informed him stiffly. "It's just too long for around here. You seem so intent on making a good impression that I thought I'd tell you."

"You really do care about me."

"Absolutely not. I don't even want you in my car."

At her vehement protests he broke into laughter and Starr joined him a few seconds later.

"Honestly, it's next to impossible to stay upset with you."

"Why try then?" he asked softly as he reached over to run his index finger down the soft, sunbleached hair on her forearm. The whisper touch of his finger against her skin made her shiver, and she was glad her driveway came into view at that moment.

"Well," Starr said as she got out of the car, "this is it. I'll warn you it's going to be messy. Since I didn't know you'd be inviting yourself. . . ."

Ignoring her needling, he took her arm as they walked up the flagstone path. "You live here all alone?" he asked as she unlocked the front door.

"Yes." She held the screen door for him. "On all ten acres. My folks left it to me. I'm sure it's not much compared to what you're used to, but it's my own little paradise and I love it." Her face glowed as she looked out across the hilly countryside.

Whatever Trevor started to say was interrupted by the vigorous welcoming of a large dog of no discriminate species. The huge shaggy canine leaped up on his chest and began to lick his face with great affectionate swipes.

"Down, Clem," Starr ordered, but the dog was too intent on welcoming Trevor to obey.

"Clem?" Trevor questioned when he was able to extricate himself from the woolly embrace.

"Short for Clementine," Starr said as she pushed the huge mongrel outside.

"Well, well. I must say she's more affectionate than her mistress." After a few minutes of trying to brush the white hairs from his coat, Trevor gave up and tossed it on the sofa.

"She's also too trusting."

"A lovely quality in a lady," Trevor remarked as he looked around the small living room.

"A dangerous one," Starr murmured and turned away so he wouldn't see the unshed tears brimming in her eyes.

Trevor followed her into the large country kitchen. "Wow!" he exclaimed as he gazed in delight at the ancient furnishings. "This is real Americana. I've never seen anything like it before. I'd love to plan a development like this."

Starr beamed with pride as he walked around

the room touching objects with wonder. The old cook stove that was still fueled by wood fascinated him. He examined the structure of the open hearth with amazement. "You could get a fortune for this place."

She poured iced tea from a heavy glass pitcher that had been her grandmother's. "I wouldn't take a fortune for it. You can have your modern chrome and glass monstrosities."

They carried the tea into the living room where Trevor settled himself in the old rocker before the fireplace. "You take care of this place by yourself?" he asked, sipping the tea as his curious eyes devoured the interior of the room. He knew the furniture was authentic without asking. He ran his hand over the polished surface of the lamp table. The maple wood glistened in the afternoon sun. "I thought you said everything was a mess."

Starr gave him an enigmatic smile. "Oh, that was just to scare you off—if nothing else worked."

He laughed at her refreshing candor. "Despite outward appearances, you're not all that tough, you know."

Starr sipped her tea in silence.

"Self-sufficient, yes," Trevor continued. "Tough, no. As I told you before, it's easy to see how you'd scare the thunder out of an ordinary guy."

Starr's rebuttal was cut short by the arrival of a small white cat who began to curl around Trevor's ankles.

He reached down and picked her up. "And

who is this?" he quizzed as she purred with delight before cuddling up in his lap.

Starr reached for the cat and her hand accidentally brushed Trevor's. They both forgot the cat and stared at each other for a long moment. Starr laughed, breaking the mood, and took the cat from him.

"This is P.J., one of my new arrivals. Someone dumped her off here, half-starved and scared to death. Unfortunately, you're right about me not being tough. Everyone in the county knows I take all the strays."

Trevor smiled, enjoying this side of her he hadn't seen before now. "P.J.?"

"Plain Jane," Starr said with a straight face.

He appraised the cat with a critical eye. "I wouldn't call her plain. She'll make some tom a good Mrs." He scratched P.J.'s belly as she purred in contentment.

"She's a sucker for that charm like everyone else, isn't she?" Starr jumped up from the sofa. What was wrong with her? She sounded like a shrew. "Well, Trevor Hall, if you're going to have dinner with a farm girl, you're going to have to earn it."

She glanced at his expensive shoes and slacks as he followed her to the chicken coop. She handed him a wicker basket.

"Did you ever do this?"

"Do what?" Trevor asked with a dubious look.

"See those ladies over there?" Starr pointed to the hens who were watching Trevor with some degree of trepidation.

He nodded and waited for further instructions.

Starr gave him a push toward the chickens. "Just ask them to surrender the fruits of their labor."

She watched in amusement as Trevor apprehensively approached the first hen. They stared at each other for a moment before Trevor made a mock bow.

"Excuse me, madam," he said to the indignant-looking hen, "I wonder if I might bother you for a moment."

With a quick motion he snatched the egg from beneath her.

Starr broke into laughter as she clapped her hands in delight. "You fibbed to me, Trevor. You've gathered eggs before."

He smiled as he continued his assigned chore.

Starr continued to watch him, marveling at the way he seemed to be completely at ease in her dilapidated hen house. He had rolled up his shirt sleeves after completing the egg gathering. As he walked toward her with a teasing smile on his tanned face, Starr found herself admiring his long, lean body.

"I don't have to kill Sunday dinner, too, do I?" He gave the chickens an ominous look.

Taking the basket from him, Starr laughed at his uneasiness. "You've forgotten—I'm a vegetarian."

"No, I really hadn't," he contradicted, the teasing look gone. "Are you a vegetarian because of health reasons?" They had begun to walk toward the house and he took her hand in his. For once she didn't pull away from him. His presence felt natural, comfortable.

She smiled up at him. "Although it is healthier to be a vegetarian—less chance of stroke or heart attack—my reasons are primarily moral. Did you ever look into the big brown eyes of a cow? Or worse—a calf?"

"Not too often," he admitted with a guilty grimace.

"I suppose you're one of those people who fails to associate the hamburgers he gets at McDonald's with the slaughter of a helpless animal."

Trevor didn't answer for a few seconds, weighing her statement. "Guilty," he confessed again. "I've never thought much about what I eat. And I know I shouldn't smoke. I know it harms the body."

He held the screen door for Starr as Clem came bounding from across the field. While Starr began fixing their dinner, Trevor remained outside to play fetch with Clem. As she chopped peppers for the omelet, she could hear his deep laughter as he coaxed the large dog to retrieve the stick he was tossing. Starr smiled as she listened to the dynamic, wealthy Mr. Hall playing like a young boy in her front yard. She paused, holding a strip of pepper in her hand for a thoughtful moment. Was it all an act? What was he really like behind those laughing green eyes?

A little later when she went to tell him dinner was ready, she found him sitting on the grass with an exhausted Clem in his lap. Again, the little-boy image flitted across her mind.

"Trevor, are you ready to eat?"

"Sure am!"

He disengaged himself from Clem and began the impossible task of brushing wisps of white hair from his slacks.

"Who had the most fun?" Starr asked.

"Probably me," Trevor admitted.

As he consumed the omelet liberally sprinkled with green peppers and tomatoes, Trevor eyed Starr with a new appreciation.

"This is really great. I had no idea you were such a good cook."

His praise brought a quick blush to her cheeks. "It's nothing," she murmured.

He cut open another flaky biscuit. "Modest, too. Don't tell me these are nothing. Did you ever think about running a restaurant instead of your health food store? Maybe you could combine the two." He applied a generous amount of butter to the steaming biscuit.

Starr pushed the rest of her omelet aside at the mention of the store, expecting another discourse on her inability to properly operate a business.

"No," she insisted, "I'm doing what I want to. I try to help people both in my store and as a city council member."

"I was just teasing. Which reminds me—I owe you an apology."

"About what?"

"About that stupid remark I made at the Braden property. I felt dumb when I walked in that room Wednesday night and saw you were a city council member."

"Oh," she said sweetly, enjoying his discomfort, "you mean the remark about my misdirected energies."

Trevor groaned in embarrassment. "That's the one."

"Apology accepted." The look in his green eyes was making her heart thump violently. She pushed back her chair and went to pour more tea. Trying to regain her composure, she kept her back to him. She was pouring the tea when he reached around her and gently took the pitcher from her hands.

"Starr," he began as she stood mesmerized, looking into his warm green eyes.

A soft knock at the door broke the magic of the moment, and with a disappointed sigh, Starr excused herself to answer the door.

Her heart was still beating wildly as she opened the screen door.

"Yes?" she said, and then let the door slam with a bang as she recognized her caller.

"Kevin!" she gasped. "What are you doing here?"

SIX
Past Love

Unable to believe her eyes, Starr stared through
the screen door at the smiling face.

"Aren't you going to invite me in, Starr?"

"Uh, yes, of course," she stammered as she
stepped back, allowing him to move past her.
Caught off guard, a flood of mixed emotions
arose in her.

At that moment Trevor came into the living
room and stopped short when he saw Kevin,
who seemed equally as surprised to find Starr
entertaining another man.

"I'm sorry. I didn't know you had company. I
wanted to talk to you. Privately." His statement
seemed to imply that Trevor was the intruder
rather than he.

Despite the dull roar in her head, Starr remembered the two men had not been introduced.

"Trevor, this is Kevin O'Riley. Kevin, Trevor
Hall."

They nodded curtly to each other without speaking. An awkward silence filled the room and Starr cleared her throat with a nervous cough.

Trevor picked up his jacket from the sofa and slung it over his shoulder. "Thanks for everything, Starr. Do you think you could drop me off in town?"

Hesitant, she turned questioning eyes to Kevin. "I'll just be a few minutes if you want to wait."

"Sure. Take your time." Settling on the sofa, he glanced around the room as though reacquainting himself with its decor before his gaze flickered back to Starr and Trevor.

Starr's cheeks burned as she brushed past Trevor to get her purse from the bedroom. She wondered if he knew that Kevin was the man who had jilted her.

They rode in silence. Starr kept her eyes on the road, not even attempting to explain Kevin's presence to Trevor. It was bad enough that their comfortable, newfound intimacy had been destroyed by Kevin's unexpected arrival.

Trevor studied her tense profile in the bright afternoon sunlight. She was biting her bottom lip as she unconsciously fought the inner turmoil of seeing Kevin in the flesh again.

"That's the old boyfriend, I take it," he commented finally in a light tone.

"Is it that obvious?"

He smiled and looked out the window at the white pines they were whizzing past. "I didn't think he was a relative."

Starr gave a short, bitter laugh.

A few minutes later they pulled into the deserted church parking lot.

"Will you be all right?" Trevor asked as he leaned over and pushed a wisp of black hair back from her warm face.

"I think so." Her serious blue eyes met his. "Five years have given me a long time to think about what happened. The worst part's over now."

Placing his large hand on the side of her face, he kissed her gently. At the touch of his hand she trembled and closed her eyes. In farewell, he touched her lips with his index finger and slipped out of the car.

"Take it easy on the poor guy," he teased with a wicked wink. "With that temper of yours he won't stand much of a chance."

On the ride home Starr rubbed her cheek where Trevor's hand had rested. So many conflicting emotions ran through her mind. She mustn't trust him. She had trusted Kevin and look what had happened.

When she entered the living room, Kevin had removed his jacket and was drinking a glass of iced tea. A momentary flash of anger filled her at his presumption of making himself at home. It was not the old days and he had no right to assume he was welcome in her home. Without speaking, she sat down across from him in the wing chair and waited.

"I'm sorry that I barged in, Starr. I always seem to be upsetting your life in one way or another."

She felt like telling him that that was the understatement of all time, but she held her silence.

"You're even more beautiful than I remembered." His eyes traveled from her long, graceful legs up to the ebony cloud of windswept hair. "Beautiful," he repeated as his eyes devoured her wholesome features. "You look as fresh as a Georgia peach."

"What do you want, Kevin?" Her voice was icy, controlled.

"How about a smile?"

"I'm afraid I have nothing to smile about as far as you're concerned. Now if you'll get on with it, I have a lot to do yet this afternoon."

She crossed her legs, leaned back in the chair, and waited for the explanation of his unannounced visit.

"Are you seriously interested in that, uh, long-haired fellow? I guess he's handsome in a way but he doesn't seem like your type...."

"I don't believe my relationship with Mr. Hall concerns you, Kevin." Outwardly she was the perfect image of the ice queen, but inside she was raging. How dare he interrogate her? Five years ago he had left without a word and now he had the nerve to sit in her house and question her taste in male friends!

Sighing in exasperation, he ran a hand through his dark hair. "You're not making this any easier," he complained.

She gave him a taut smile. "Why should I?"

He spread his hands in a gesture of defeat.

"All right, I'm sorry again. I didn't come here to make you angry."

"I'm not angry." Her clipped words belied her statement.

"Oh, Starr, you'll never know how I regret what I did to you every day of my life. I was so wrong. How you must hate me." He dropped his head into his hands and sat in silent misery.

She stared at him, feeling nothing. There had been a time when she would have longed to hear him say that he was sorry, that he had made a terrible mistake. Now all she felt was a dead weight in her chest where her heart should have been.

The silence stretched on and Starr shifted impatiently in the chair. "Did you come here for a specific reason, Kevin?"

He raised his head and she saw unshed tears glistening in his dark eyes. "I came here to ask you to forgive me, Starr. I realize what I did to you is really unforgivable. But I want you to know that I still love you and always will."

Shocked at his unexpected confession, she continued to stare at him. How could he speak of love? She stood up and opened an antique music box on the mantel as she fought to control her anger. The lilting tune filled the room as she turned to accuse him.

"Love?" Her usually soft voice vibrated in the room. "What could you know of love, Kevin?" Her blue eyes were dark with anger. "Love goes hand in hand with trust, and that's something I could never feel for you again. Or any other man.

Don't talk to me about love," she said through clenched teeth.

"Starr, listen to me," he pleaded as he grasped her shoulders. "I know that running away and leaving you to face all those people was terrible, but I was afraid of getting tied down, of losing my freedom. It was never a question of wanting to hurt you. I was just scared."

Starr brusquely shook off his hands and sat down again. Her head was spinning in confusion. "Is that what you came here to tell me?"

"Yes. And to ask for your forgiveness."

Starr remained silent, thinking of the years of hurt he had inflicted on her.

"You will forgive me, won't you, Starr? I mean really forgive me."

"You're forgiven, Kevin," she told him in a flat, unemotional voice. "Now, if you'll excuse me, I have some chores awaiting me."

Hurrying from the house, she went to mix the chicken feed, glad for something to keep her hands busy. Why had he shown up after all these years? Her lips had spoken forgiveness, but in her heart the feelings of the resentment, the anger, the hurt that permeated her soul were still there. She heard his car pull out of the driveway and breathed a sigh of relief.

Whistling an off-key tune, she poured her energy into cleaning the barn. She heard a soft bleating and turned around to find Excalibur watching her.

"Hi, girl. Like my whistling? Proves you're a real connoisseur." The goat chewed contentedly as she watched Starr rake the hay. One of the roosters wandered into the barn and peered curiously at her.

"Well, Reveille, what do you think of the situation?"

He flapped his wings and strutted out of the door.

"Men!" Starr exclaimed, shaking her head in disgust.

The next afternoon Starr sat in Jan's living room telling her about Kevin's sudden return. It was one of the only times in the past few days she'd been able to find Jan at home.

"You've been seeing a lot of Bob Mason, haven't you?" she asked, trying to keep the jealousy from her voice. It wasn't like Jan to spend her time with someone else. And she'd been the one who had talked Jan into going out with Bob in the first place. Served her right. That's what she deserved for playing Cupid.

Jan blushed to match her hair. "Yes, I have. He's...."

"Wonderful," Starr supplied in a dry tone as Jan nodded in complete agreement.

"Yes, I guess I have to admit it."

Melissa and Frank were watching television and Starr gazed at the set with an absent-minded stare.

"Did Kevin ask to see you again?" Jan ventured.

"I didn't really give him a chance to ask. I don't want to see him."

"I've heard that he was married and divorced since he left Springfield."

"Marvelous. That certainly makes his vow of undying love suspect."

It was Jan's turn to be surprised. "Is he still in love with you?"

"So he says. He wants my forgiveness."

Jan mopped at a damp ring on the end table where Melissa's milk had been resting. "Did you forgive him?"

"I told him I did."

"Ah, but I suspect you didn't." She studied her best friend's closed eyes as if trying to read what lay behind those very private barriers.

"I don't know that I can. Jesus said we should forgive seventy times seven and here I am having trouble with one times one. It's been five years, Jan, but the hurt is still like yesterday."

"I know." There was little to say that she hadn't already said in an effort to comfort Starr.

"Trevor Hall was at the house when Kevin came by."

"Oh, my. I bet that proved interesting."

"Sort of. Kevin didn't really like to see a strange man in my living room. What makes him think he can walk back into my life after five years and act like he has rights?"

"How did Trevor react?"

"Like a gentleman. He excused himself politely and left me to hassle with Kevin—after I had taken him back to church."

Jan raised a questioning eyebrow. "What? I

must have missed part of the story somewhere."

Starr briefly explained the confrontation at church. By the time she'd finished the story, Jan was smiling.

"You two do seem doomed to run into each other."

"More like a head-on collision," Starr corrected. "He always gets under my skin. I don't know how he manages to get me in an uproar without even trying."

A knowing look flickered in Jan's eyes. "Well, what's that old saying about opposites attract?"

"They may attract but they sure clash in our case."

"I think if you would really let yourself, Starr, you and Trevor—"

"No!" Starr interrupted in such a loud voice that Frank and Melissa turned shocked eyes in her direction. She smiled quickly to assure them that everything was all right. "I mean, he's not the kind of man I care to know any better."

Jan forced back a smile at Starr's vehement protests. "Well, I sure like Bob."

Starr paused, her cup of tea midway to her lips. "Is it serious?" she asked in a small, quiet voice.

Jan thought for a moment. "I like him. I don't want to think any further than that right now." Her eyes grew misty. "He's the first man I've been able to talk to since Frank—" she was unable to finish the sentence and Starr looked down at the floor, wanting to absorb the hurt that still plagued Jan even after all this time.

"Is Kevin staying around town?"

Starr shrugged, her gesture indicating her lack of interest.

Jan frowned. "I hope he's not planning on staying here permanently."

Again Starr shrugged. "Who cares?" Although her tone was flip, Jan could detect the pain that lurked dangerously close to the surface.

When the doorbell rang, they were watching the evening news.

"Bob!" Starr heard Jan exclaim, the delight obvious in her tone. Frank and Melissa hopped down from the sofa and ran to greet him, as excited as their mother. From the couch Starr could see Bob hand them each a small box as they shrieked in uncontained excitement.

"Oh, Bob, you shouldn't have," Jan protested lamely as the children rushed to open their gifts.

"Come in the front room," Jan coaxed as she pulled him after her. "Starr's here."

He stood awkwardly in the center of the small room as Jan hustled around getting him a cup of coffee.

As she looked into his warm, friendly eyes, Starr felt her resentment at his intrusion dissolve. Her tiny pangs of jealousy vanished as she realized how lucky Jan was to have met someone like Bob. Shyly, Bob seated himself across from Starr.

"How's your land development coming along?" Starr inquired. Her question sounded more prying than she had intended.

A guilty look flashed into his eyes. "I know

you don't approve of what Trevor's doing, Miss Monroe, but there are a lot of good things that will result from it in the long run." His earnest brown eyes pled for understanding.

"I'm sure." Her sarcasm was thinly veiled. What did she expect? Trevor Hall was the kind of man who would demand and receive fierce loyalty from his employees. It certainly hadn't taken him long to win over the city council.

Jan appeared with Bob's coffee and sat next to him.

"Trevor has gone deeply into debt to finance this job. If it doesn't work out—" Bob spread his hands in a helpless gesture.

Starr sipped her tea thoughtfully, her curiosity aroused. "Are you saying that he could 'belly up,' as they say in financial circles, if this project isn't approved?"

Bob frowned. "Trevor's quite diversified, but—"

Jan shot Starr a warning glare. "Let's talk about something else," she suggested.

Starr heeded Jan's signal and shut up immediately. It wasn't long before she felt like the proverbial fifth wheel. They seemed to forget she was even in the room. Excusing herself with a plea of tiredness, she left after kissing Frank and Melissa good-night.

On her way out, she glanced back to Bob and Jan who were sitting together on the sofa gazing at each other with unabashed admiration. Starr shook her head in disbelief. Honestly, she would have thought Jan was much too levelheaded to get that moonstruck look in her eyes.

She drove slowly toward home, enjoying the sights and smells of the ending day. The days would soon be growing shorter and autumn would suddenly appear one crisp morning without warning. Overnight the carpet of green would turn to gold and the rolling hills would be ablaze with color. The sun dropped suddenly behind a tall mountain and Starr shivered. Fear twisted in her chest as she thought of Jan and Bob Mason. If Jan became seriously interested in him, she might be leaving Springfield when Trevor's housing project was completed. If the project was completed, she corrected herself. And Trevor, too, might leave, she suddenly realized. For a moment his teasing green eyes danced before her, willing her to think about him.

Long shadows were touching the peaceful hills when she pulled into her driveway. Clem came bounding around the side of the house, agog with excitement, to see her.

"Hungry, girl?" she asked as she affectionately rubbed the big dog's ears. It was almost dark before all the animals were fed and she was at last able to prepare her own meager evening meal. She stood at the sink looking out across the meadow, as she spread chunky peanut butter on the last of her homemade bread. *What was it Trevor had said about me? Oh, yes, he could see me making peanut butter sandwiches for my own little brood.* She screwed the lid back on the jar with a vicious twist. Once and for all she was going to put him out of her mind. It was bad enough that her knees turned to rubber every time he kissed her.

"Wrong again, Trevor," she muttered angrily. "Good grief, P.J., he's got me talking to myself." She carried her sandwich and glass of milk into the living room as P.J. trailed along behind, meowing every step of the way.

Starr had just finished her sandwich and was watching a documentary on disappearing natural resources when a knock sounded at the door.

"Just a minute," she called as she switched on the small lamp by the sofa. When she turned on the outside light, she was surprised to see Kevin fighting off Clem.

"Get this beast away from me," he pleaded as Clem growled deep in her throat and clung tenaciously to his pant leg.

Starr broke into helpless laughter at the stricken look on his face. "It's all right, girl. You can let go now," she assured the shaggy dog as she opened the door to admit Kevin.

"Really, Starr," he complained as he followed her into the living room, "that dog is a menace. It ought to be tied up."

Motioning for him to be seated, she smiled. She had forgotten how Kevin disliked animals, especially dogs.

"She's a baby," Starr insisted. "And she's a terrific guard dog. She wouldn't do me much good tied up."

"Well," he admitted reluctantly as he sat down, "I suppose a woman living alone in the country needs some kind of protection." He crossed his legs and attempted to brush away the animal hair that clung to his dark pants.

Suppressing another smile, Starr watched his slim fingers pick nervously at the offending hairs. She looked down at her own well-worn jeans. She was around the animals so much she never bothered to check her clothes. In the soft glow of the setting sun she studied Kevin. His curly brown hair was clipped neat and in the latest fashion. As he gazed around her living room, his thin lips curled with just the slightest hint of disapproval for her odd taste in furnishings. She saw him now with new eyes, older eyes. Had she really thought she wanted to marry him?

"You're not the same, Starr," he said, with disappointment reflected in both his speech and his eyes.

Her lips curved in an almost invisible smile. "I should hope not, Kevin. I wouldn't want to be the same person I was five years ago. I think God wants us to grow and learn, not just pass through life." She finished her milk as P.J. landed in her lap.

"Beat you," she teased the small cat, and raced toward the kitchen to rinse her glass. Poor Kevin would probably die of shock if he saw P.J. trying to lick her glass.

Starr was running water in the glass when Kevin came up behind her and slid his arms around her waist. At his touch she instantly froze.

"Starr, I still love you," he whispered against the back of her neck. "I've never been able to forget you. Can't you give me another chance?"

She struggled in his embrace, only to find herself more firmly trapped. "Let me go, Kevin," she demanded. She disliked the desperate pleading almost as much as his unwanted embrace.

The pressure of his arms slackened momentarily and Starr managed to break free. "Please, Kevin," she asked in a trembling voice as she backed away from him, "please leave right now. This has gone too far already."

"You heard the lady," a soft, firm voice said from the doorway. Trevor's tall frame filled the room.

Starr stared at him with a dumbfounded expression. Vaguely aware of Clem's scratching and whining outside the kitchen door, she wondered how Trevor had materialized from nowhere.

As Kevin stepped away from her, he glared at Trevor. "Listen, this is between Starr and me. Why don't you just mind your own business?"

Trevor flipped on the light switch, bathing them all suddenly in a warm yellow glow. Starr shuddered as she looked into his eyes. They glowed like icy emeralds as he faced Kevin.

"I believe Miss Monroe has asked you to leave." His voice was calm and controlled, but Starr could see the dangerous glint in his flashing eyes. "I would advise you to do as she has requested."

Embarrassed by the whole situation, Starr turned her back on both men and stared out the kitchen window. For five years she had lived without male companionship. Now all of a sudden she needed a traffic signal to maintain order in her own kitchen.

She heard the front door open and shut with an angry bang, then Clem's threatening growl, and Trevor's soft voice telling the dog everything was all right.

When she turned around, Trevor was standing by the door watching her with a concerned expression.

"You always seem to show up at the most unexpected times," she said in sharp rebuke.

His eyes narrowed in anger. "I would have thought from the situation you were in when I arrived, that you would be grateful I did show up."

"I can take care of myself."

"Well, fine," he exploded. "Pardon me for interfering, Miss Monroe. Perhaps you'll be lucky enough to get jilted again."

The color drained from her face. "Get out!" she screamed at him as she threw the nearest thing she could lay her hand on. Fortunately for Trevor it turned out to be a potholder.

In the confusion, Clem burst through the door, which Trevor had just flung open in anger. P.J. jumped on top of the refrigerator, knocking over the cookie jar. And Trevor tripped over Clem, who was making a wild dash for the cookies that were rolling across the kitchen floor.

Starr's anger quickly evaporated as she watched the chaotic scene. Trevor lay sprawled on the floor as Clem climbed across his inert body to gobble the errant cookies. Starr laughed until her side was twisted in agony. Her breath came in quick, labored gasps as she tried to control the laughter.

Trevor feebly fought off Clem as she licked his face, her wide tongue leaving a trail of sticky cookie crumbs.

"Here," Starr said, offering him a paper towel. From her safe perch atop the refrigerator, P.J. watched the antics of the rest of the household. Starr took another look at Trevor and collapsed on the floor beside him. Trevor propped himself up against the refrigerator as he wiped his face. Clem sat on her haunches, wagging her tail as she surveyed the two of them from behind the tangle of hair that covered her bright eyes.

Starr reached over to touch Trevor's shirt, which had a long tear in it. "Oh, Trevor, I'm sorry."

His green eyes swept over her, lingering on the flushed cheeks and the wide blue eyes dancing with unconcealed merriment. Her thick black hair was in complete disarray, but his eyes said she was the most beautiful woman in the world. He pulled her to him and, hypnotized, she watched his lips descend until they claimed hers. A sob caught in her throat, but died as his lips tenderly dispelled her laughter.

"Have you ever been kissed before lying in front of a refrigerator with a dog and a cat watching every movement?" he quipped, easing the tension that had engulfed them.

Starr began to giggle again as she looked up to see Clem gazing at them with a quizzical expression, her tail thumping happily on the floor.

Trevor continued to hold her as his strong fingers cut into the firm flesh of her upper arms.

"I bet you never found anything this romantic in California," she teased.

"Right," he agreed as his green eyes grew serious.

The look in his eyes frightened her and Starr suddenly jumped up, shooing Clem and P.J. out of the kitchen.

"I'm sorry about your shirt," she apologized as she helped him brush the cookie crumbs from his clothes.

"Don't worry about it," he murmured as he pulled her into his arms once again. He felt her trembling in his embrace. "Starr," he whispered as he rained butterfly kisses on her face, "do you still love him?"

Her knees continued to tremble, but her thoughts were not of Kevin.

He tilted her chin, searching her eyes for the answer.

"No, I don't think I ever did," she admitted.

At her answer, his lips happily sought hers once more. Starr's arms tightened around his lean waist and she nestled close in the haven of his embrace.

"Good," he whispered against her lips. "Good."

SEVEN
Revelations

The following morning Starr stood at the kitchen counter staring out the window and thinking of Trevor. A wisp of merriment twitched at her lips as she recalled the riotous scene that had transpired in her kitchen the previous evening. Now she realized she had been wrong in attacking him verbally for coming to her defense; but pride had made her strike out at him.

"Oh, Trevor," she sighed as she tried to force herself to return to the present. The council meeting was tomorrow night and a final vote was needed for him to continue with his housing development. Confusion gripped her mind. Part of her wanted to vote for him and the other part clung firmly to past values. Maybe it wouldn't be so bad if Trevor completed his project. Springfield's ailing economy would certainly benefit. Deep in thought, it took her a few seconds to realize that the phone was ringing. She raced to the living room to answer it.

"Good morning, gorgeous," a deep voice whispered in her ear.

Starr's knees weakened at the sound of his rich baritone purring in her ear. "Good morning," she managed to stammer as she remembered his ardent kisses.

"How's Clem this morning?"

She suppressed a giggle that rose at the mention of the large mutt. "She's fine. Not too hungry."

"I guess not," Trevor laughed. "I think that dog has a real sweet tooth. You'd better give her a lecture on manners as well as nutrition. She eats like she's starving."

"She's already heard all my lectures. Besides, the cookies didn't have sugar in them."

"Oh. Yummy like the tea, huh?"

Starr laughed softly into the receiver as she pictured his teasing green eyes.

"You just wait, Trevor Hall. I'll reform you yet."

"That's why I'm calling. I'll take you to dinner tonight and eat anything you order for me."

"Promise?"

"Well, anything but sprouts."

"Always the typical businessman—compromising already."

"Have to. You drive a hard bargain, Miss Monroe. I'll pick you up tonight around six."

A dreamy lassitude engulfed Starr as she hung

up the phone. Her usual high energy level had disappeared. She sighed and stared out the kitchen window as the warm August breeze ruffled the crisp white curtains. This wasn't like her at all. If she hadn't known better, she would have thought spring was just around the corner. She had lain awake half the night reliving Trevor's kisses, remembering the tender look in his bewitching green eyes.

Poor Kevin hadn't rated more than a passing thought, and then only a fleeting moment of anger at his unexpected behavior. How strange that Trevor had shown up when he did. Kevin's amorous overtures had surprised and shocked her. And he had the nerve to accuse her of changing!

Finishing her tea and toast, Starr hurried to get ready for work. The day threatened to be another hot one. She slipped into red cotton slacks and a red and white sleeveless blouse. Pulling her long dark hair back into a ponytail, she tied it with a red ribbon.

At the store, the morning passed slowly and Starr found herself gazing into space more than once as she thought about Trevor. A few minutes after noon she called Jan to ask her to lunch. She was told that Jan had already left with a gentleman friend.

"Well!" Starr exclaimed to the empty store. "I've evidently been stood up for Bob Mason." She didn't really mind. It was wonderful to see Jan living in the present again.

She ate a container of plain yogurt and thought of how Trevor would tease her if he saw her choice of luncheon fare.

"I must quit this," she chastised herself for the hundredth time. "I'm not a teenager with a crush."

She was in the back room sorting stock when she heard the tinkle of the bell.

"Just a minute," she called, wiping her hands on a paper towel. When she turned around, Trevor was standing in the door watching her.

The look in his eyes made her blush.

"How long have you been standing there?" she asked as she crumpled the towel.

"Not long enough," he said quietly.

"I didn't expect to see you until tonight." She started to move around him to enter the shop, but he reached out and pulled her into his arms.

"Trevor," she protested. "What if someone comes in?"

"Hmm," he murmured as he bent to kiss her trembling lips. Starr was powerless to resist him. Her arms slipped around his neck and she returned his kiss with reckless abandon.

"Whoa, little lady," Trevor teased, breaking the embrace and pushing her reluctantly away. "You're much too tempting as it is."

Starr felt the warmth suffuse her cheeks. "I'm sorry," she whispered in mortification. This feeling was so new to her. She'd never responded to Kevin like that.

He tilted her chin and gazed for a long moment into her vivid blue eyes. "I came by to tell you that I've moved from the hotel in Pixley to an apartment here in town."

Her heart pounded with excitement at his news. "So you can be closer to your work?" she asked with an impish grin.

"No," Trevor said, tweaking her nose, "so I can be closer to you."

"Oh," Starr said in a breathless whisper.

The bell chimed and she started reluctantly toward the front of the store.

"Oh, there you are, Starr," Jan said and broke off with a knowing smile as she spotted Trevor. "Sorry I had already gone to lunch. Bob took me to the café. Hi, Trevor."

Trevor chatted with Jan for a few minutes before leaving. On his way out, he winked at Starr.

"See you later, Miss Monroe."

After Trevor had gone, Jan smiled at Starr. "Well, this looks pretty serious to me."

"He came by to tell me he's moved into town."

Jan nodded. "He and Bob are sharing an apartment. They're renting from Mrs. Howard on Marshall Avenue."

They drank cold grape juice and watched the sparse traffic on Main Street.

"Are you serious about Bob?" Starr asked Jan.

Her brown eyes danced with joy. "Let's just say I'm happier than I've been in a long time. And the kids are crazy about him. I never expected to be happy again."

Starr squeezed her hand. "I know."

"Still upset with Trevor about the project?"

Starr sighed and tossed the cup into the wastebasket. "The council meeting is tomorrow night. I'll have to make up my mind by then. I prayed about it last night. I did a lot of talking and God did a lot of listening but—" She shrugged and spread her hands in a gesture of defeat. "I guess the Lord wants me to figure this one out for myself."

Jan laughed in empathy. "It would help if Trevor were a nasty old codger, wouldn't it?"

"It certainly would," she agreed.

Shortly before five she closed the store and drove by the construction site. She was startled at how rapidly the area had changed. Despite the heat of the late afternoon sun, she shivered as she stood on the small knoll overlooking the property. The virgin land lay exposed, brutally stripped of its trees and greenery.

Starr thought of the hours she and her youth group had spent raising money for their reclamation of a strip mining area north of town. Replanting the damaged area had been her idea, but the teenage group had enthusiastically welcomed the hard work necessary to raise the money. Slowly but surely the funds had come in from bake sales, car washes, rummage sales, and whatever else they could figure out to get more money.

This spring they had finally been able to plant thousands of flowers in the area so badly scarred by the so-called advances of technology and progress. They had dragged their bags of peat moss, bone meal, and gypsum out to the site on a beautiful spring day. At the end of the day, thousands of yellow daffodils, grape hyacinths, marigolds, and blue-violet ageratum plants had graced the once unsightly spot.

She gazed sadly at the raw earth as a big bulldozer groaned in the heat. Now here was another eyesore in the name of progress. And this time she doubted that there was anything she could do to reverse the damage. Trevor Hall was a strong man used to getting what he wanted. He wasn't all wrong, of course. She could see what the development could do for the town. Maybe she was old-fashioned and out of tune, but still she longed to see the land unspoiled by man's handiwork. Trevor's accusation that first night was probably right. She wasn't very progressive.

She drove along the quiet back road toward home, thinking of how much her life had changed since she'd met Trevor Hall. For the first time since Kevin had walked out of her life, she felt alive again. Maybe too much, she conceded, as a soft blush tainted her bronze cheeks.

"I need help, Lord," she whispered. "I'm too strongly attracted to this man for my own good." As she turned in the driveway, Clem bounded up the path to greet her with an enthusiastic bark.

"Hi, baby," Starr said as she scratched the long, floppy ears. "You're hot, aren't you, sweetheart?"

Without bothering to change her clothes, she hurried to feed her menagerie. Trevor would be picking her up in less than an hour.

After a quick shower, Starr rummaged desperately through her small closet looking for something attractive to wear.

"Terrible," she said in disgust as she tossed her choice aside on the already cluttered bed. Nothing she had was extra special. "Well, Starr," she lectured herself, "that's what you get for closing yourself off from life all these years."

She pulled more items from her sparse closet, looking at each one with a critical eye. She did have that one navy blue dress she always wore to council meetings, but it was so matronly looking. She heard Trevor pull in the driveway and a horror-stricken look crossed her face. Oh, no, he's here and I haven't found anything to wear yet!

Wearing her robe and a miserable expression, she answered the door.

Trevor looked cool and crisp in a soft gray suit and a red shirt.

"Am I early?" he asked as he glanced at her robe.

"No. I can't find anything to wear."

"Women," he said with a knowing grimace, and shook his head in mock disgust.

"I'm serious, Trevor. I don't own anything but jeans and slacks. I never think about clothes."

He leaned over to kiss her cheek. "I know. That's one of the things I find so refreshing about you, Starr. You're not like most women, always concerned with the outer wrappings, always worried about their hair, their makeup, their wardrobes."

She smiled at his compliment. "My parents always encouraged me to develop my mind. I guess I'm a lot like those nuns who never look in a mirror."

"You should," Trevor said in a husky whisper. "You'd find a beautiful lady looking back."

Blushing, she excused herself to go get dressed. She finally decided to wear the same blue dress she'd worn for their first disastrous dinner engagement. This time it would be different.

As they drove away, a soulful-eyed Clem sat on the front porch, sadly gazing after them.

Trevor glanced back at her in the rearview mirror. "Did you tell her we'd bring her a doggy bag?"

Starr gave him a suspicious look. "So you're already deciding not to eat what I order for you."

"You know, you should have given serious consideration to being a lawyer or a private detective. You don't miss a thing, do you, Sherlock?"

He took her to a small restaurant on the outskirts of town that featured a live band and dancing. Trevor was delighted with the rustic decor of the restaurant. Barrels had been hollowed out, shellacked, and made into chairs. Corn husks and gaily colored gourds hung from the side walls.

"Is this down-home enough for you?" Starr teased.

"This is a fantastic place. I've never seen a decor quite like this." His eyes glowed with appreciation for the country atmosphere.

From behind the large menu, Starr studied him with covert glances. He looked up suddenly and caught her inquisitive gaze.

"You're really an enigma," she told him.

"Why is that, doctor?"

"Because," she said, folding the menu, "you appear to be very modern, very sophisticated— but the things you really seem to admire are old and rustic."

He smiled and folded his menu without commenting on her observation. "Well, what am I eating, Miss Monroe?"

With a little coaching from her he ordered the halibut brochette.

They were just finishing dinner when Trevor took her hand. "Starr, I wanted to be alone with you tonight because I have something I need to tell you."

Her eyes were glued to his and she felt her heart quicken at his words. She could hear the music and the soft purr of conversation around them, but he alone seemed to exist at that moment. Everyone else in the room suddenly disappeared as she gazed into his warm green eyes.

"Yes," she whispered, unable to say more than that one simple word.

"When I first saw you, Starr Monroe, I thought you were a stubborn, opinionated, bleeding-heart liberal. And a troublemaker, too," he added. "But then after I got to know you better, I saw what a beautiful person you are inside and out. What I'm trying to say and doing a lousy job of, is that I'm in love with you."

Starr sat very still as the blood pounding in her ears all but obliterated the sound of the band.

Trevor raised her hand to his lips and kissed her fingers, one by one. Turning her hand over, he kissed the inside of her wrist. She continued to gaze at him with a stunned expression.

He laughed softly. "Do you know when I knew for sure?"

She shook her head.

"It was the Sunday you brought Jan's children to the construction site. I saw you holding Melissa in your arms and I was so entranced with the picture you two made, I knew you had to be the future mother of my children. Our children," he corrected.

"Children?" Starr stammered finally.

Trevor laughed again and squeezed her hand with a possessive grip. "You do want children, don't you? I can't imagine a marriage without them." His voice softened as he gazed at her. "I can't imagine you without them. God intended for you to be a mother. A wonderful one."

Starr recovered her voice at last. "I'm still trying to adjust to the idea of your loving me and you already have us with children," she complained in a nervous rush of laughter.

"Well, I'm thirty-four, Starr. I don't want to wait forever to play with my sons."

The idea took her breath away, as she thought of sons who looked like Trevor. Little blond boys with mischievous green eyes. Maybe a daughter with black hair.

Tears slid quietly down her cheeks and Trevor

wiped them away with a napkin.

"I still don't approve of what you're doing to the Braden property," she sniffled in protest. She had to retain some of her pride at least.

"I know, honey," he said as he wiped away the last trace of her tears. "I hope to change your mind about that."

When they left the restaurant, the August night was still sultry and heavy with humidity. They drove along the back roads listening to the radio.

Trevor pulled the car into the construction site.

"What are we doing here?" Starr asked as he helped her out of the car.

Smiling mysteriously, he pulled her along after him. In the soft light of the summer moon the giant bulldozers and earthmovers loomed dark and foreboding, like ancient ruins. Trevor showed her around the site after warning her to watch out for nails and other scattered building materials. They sat on a wooden horse and watched the moon floating high in the peaceful heavens. Far above, the brilliant stars twinkled like faraway diamonds, elusive, teasing.

"I always wanted to build," Trevor began in a soft voice. "Working with my hands has been a great joy in my life. My dad was a very successful builder, maybe too much so." Bitterness had crept into his voice for a moment. "He and my mother divorced when I was in high school."

"Oh, Trevor, I'm sorry," Starr whispered and covered his large hand with hers.

"I went through an awful time when they

divorced. Smoked marijuana, drank anything with an alcoholic content, skipped school. I couldn't believe my world had fallen apart."

Starr continued to hold his hand, feeling his hurt.

"In the end one of my friends convinced me I needed help and literally dragged me to church with him. I was living with my mother at the time and hating my father for what he had done to our lives. I was really skeptical about going. You know—what had God done for me lately? Let the two people I loved most in the world grow bitter toward each other."

Starr felt tears burn her eyelids. It had been hard to lose her own parents so early in life, but at least she had known they loved each other until the end.

They sat in silence for a while as the sultry August night finally yielded to the cooling night wind. The huge bulldozers and earthmovers sat like silent sentinels, glowing yellowish-orange in the brilliant moonlight. Trevor slipped an arm around Starr's shoulder as she shivered.

"So in desperation you turned at last to God?" she asked, as she gazed at his shadowed profile.

"I was at the bottom of the pit, hating everyone. Most of all my parents, for what they had done to me. I was so filled with my needs, my wants, that I never stopped to think what it must have done to them. Until that night in church I had never thought too much about anyone but myself. I guess I thought everyone was just like me."

Starr squeezed his hand. "A lot of people are

concerned only with themselves," she agreed. "I guess that's why I'm such a do-gooder, as I've often been termed, and not too kindly. So many people don't care about anything but their own personal gratification. It's only when you help other people that you really understand what Christ was trying to teach."

"I went to church that night with my best friend, Harold Miller," Trevor continued, "expecting nothing, caring about nothing. The world had turned sour for me at sixteen. But when I walked into that little old-fashioned church and saw those words over the altar, something happened to me." His voice had grown husky with remembrance.

"What words?" Starr asked curiously.

"God is love."

"And did you accept him in your life then?"

"From that moment on."

A pang of guilt stabbed Starr suddenly. "I called you money hungry."

Trevor laughed. "Being a good Christian and a good businessman is sometimes awfully hard, Starr. I'm sure a lot of people have thought I was nuts over the years with some of the decisions I've made. I don't stand on the corner with my sign reading 'Christian at Work,' but I have quietly tried to do what I could."

A warm glow of happiness spread through Starr as she listened to Trevor. She had been so wrong about him. So wrong.

"Trevor," she whispered his name in the moonlight, but his lips silenced hers before she could voice her thoughts. She trembled in delight in his strong arms as the kiss deepened in intensity. He pulled back from her and studied her face in the glow of the moonlight.

"Starr, I love you. I've never said that to another woman except my mother. I've always been afraid, I guess, of getting hurt. I didn't want to wind up like my mom and dad, bitter, resentful of the wasted years with someone who no longer cared."

An awesome feeling swept over her as she stared up into his eyes. The hard little knot in her throat refused to go away no matter how often she swallowed. It seemed impossible that this man she had detested a few days ago was offering his love to her. She tugged at the blond hair that skimmed his shirt collar with trembling fingers.

"Still don't like my hair?" he teased.

Burying her fingers in the thick strands, she murmured, "I love it. I was mad at you that Sunday because you made me look a little too honestly at myself."

He pulled her close again. "When you're mad, your eyes sparkle like blue dynamite. When I kissed you that first night after taking you to dinner, I was surprised that you didn't slug me." He laughed, his lips pressed against the thick black cloud of her hair.

"Would you have turned the other cheek?"

"Yes," Trevor admitted, much to her delight.

Starr slid her arm around his waist. "You mean underneath that fierce macho image is a big pussycat?"

"A pushover," he confessed. "But then how

many of us are what we appear to be?" With a lightning alacrity his mood had changed.

"What do you mean?" Something in his tone bothered her. Did he mean her specifically?

Trevor's soft laughter filled the warm night. "I mean, dear heart, that there are depths in most of us that are seldom seen by even our closest friends. You, for example, hide behind that facade of a strong-willed, independent woman to frighten off any interested male. That way you don't have to face any emotional involvement."

A protest rose to her lips, but Trevor silenced it almost immediately with a kiss.

"But," he continued, pulling her off the wooden horse, "you didn't fool me. Not even for one minute."

As he picked out a clean path through the construction debris, Starr smiled to herself and followed him toward the car.

She snuggled close to him as he drove slowly through the moonlit hills. Her heart was filled to overflowing. A soft sigh of contentment escaped from her and she glanced up at Trevor's lean profile silhouetted against the moonlight.

He returned her smile with such a look of tenderness that she thought her heart would break from happiness. Thank you, Lord, she prayed silently. For so long the world had appeared to be a bleak place, but now....

She touched his cheek with her fingers, trailing down to the nape of his neck where the thick blond hair curled softly. But now Trevor had changed her life in such a short time. She rested her head against the seat as the breeze gently tugged at her long hair.

Starr was sure her life would never be the same again.

EIGHT
Gentle
Evening

Sleep eluded Starr as she listened to the wind whistling through the leaves of the oak tree outside her bedroom window. Her heart sang a happy refrain that began and ended with Trevor. All the time she had thought he was arrogant, money hungry, and uncaring. What a pleasant surprise to find he had accepted Christ so early in his life. Her heart went out to him as she thought of the hurt and frustration he must have suffered during that tumultuous time after his parents had separated.

"What God has joined together," she whispered, and Kevin's image popped into her mind. If she had married Kevin, what a mistake it would have been. God in his infinite wisdom had spared her much heartache.

Hugging her pillow, she smiled into the darkness, thinking of Trevor. How wrong she had been about him. Drowsiness finally overcame her excitement and she fell asleep with a happy smile on her lips and Trevor's green eyes dancing in her dreams.

Neither Clem's loud snoring on the floor at the foot of her bed nor P.J.'s tramping across her chest to cuddle up beside her, bothered her pleasant dreams.

Sunlight bathed her face with warm caresses when her eyes opened the next morning.

"Oh, my gosh, P.J.," she said, jumping out of bed and dashing around the room. "I forgot to set the alarm last night."

P.J. didn't seem too upset about the situation as she stretched languidly in the morning sunshine and yawned. Starr quickly showered and was frantically trying to pull on her slacks when Clem appeared at the bedroom door carrying her plastic bowl.

"Oh, Clem, I'm late. I don't have time to feed you right now."

The big dog dropped the bowl and lay down in the doorway.

Starr laughed as she brushed her tangled hair, trying to force it into some kind of order. "Are you on a sit-down protest? Unfair conditions, huh? Or is it a lie-down demonstration?"

She stepped over the huge dog after quickly scratching one ear. Hurrying to the kitchen, she put the teakettle on the burner for a quick cup of tea. She felt the bowl hit the back of her legs.

"All right, I give up," she conceded with a sigh and pulled out the large sack of dog food from the cupboard. By the time she had carried the bowl to the front porch, the kettle was whistling. She could hear Clem crunching her dry dog food.

As she stood at the counter stirring honey into the peppermint tea, her thoughts returned to Trevor and the events of the past evening.

"P.J.," she called as she poured a saucer of milk and waited for the young cat to come running, "hurry up, girl. I'm late and I'm leaving in two minutes."

She pushed Trevor out of her mind. She had a business to run. Although she was late, she drove slowly through the twisting hills. The morning sun warmed the dark pines with long golden rays as the hills came to life for another day. Starr often thought of King David as she drove the rugged terrain of the land she loved so well. Their sheer beauty made her want to break into song—no wonder David had been able to compose so many of his psalms as he sat beside the still waters of a mountain stream. Nowhere was God more in evidence than here in these rugged green mountains.

Maybe it was hard for Trevor to understand why she wanted the land left as it was. It was just as difficult for her to understand why he wanted to deface it with man-made structures. She tried to blot out the image of the Braden place with the large construction equipment busy at work tearing up the lush greenery of the tranquil surroundings. Although it hadn't looked so bad at night. Maybe she was wrong. Perhaps there were times when the end justified the means.

She was disappointed when Trevor failed to call during the day. A steady flow of customers in the morning kept her busy and she spent the afternoon marking stock. The temperature had dropped suddenly and fall could be felt in the air. A new fear tugged at her heart. Would Trevor be leaving when his construction crew could no longer work?

She stood motionless for a long moment, staring into space. She was afraid to think too far ahead into the future. After all, it was still a long time until winter, and Indian summer would afford extra days for building. But when winter finally came, would he be leaving? Suddenly it became very important that he stay in Springfield.

In order to get home and finish her chores before the council meeting, she closed the shop earlier than usual. Even with that, she was five minutes late as she slid into her seat with apologies to the mayor and the rest of the council. They agreed unanimously to try to raise funds to open the city swimming pool for the next season. No one really had any good ideas on how to do it, so they shelved the fund-raising aspect after appointing a committee to work out the details.

When they came to the Hall project, Starr held her breath. All day long she had been trying to avoid thinking about it. Where Trevor was involved, she found it hard to keep her emotions clear. She toyed with a paper clip as Mayor

Russell discussed what the development of the property would mean for the town's economy. Raising her eyes, she discovered Burton's gaze on her and quickly ducked her head again. He was impossible.

She returned her attention to the mayor as he concluded his speech. They were ready to vote. As she had known she would all along, she cast her vote in favor of the project and wasn't surprised to see the motion carried unanimously. A murmur of approval swept through the room. Starr felt strangely uneasy. A sense of having compromised her morals nagged at her.

After the meeting she hurried from the courthouse to her little VW as the wind whipped at her hair with cold fingers. Shivering from the blasts of cold air, she turned on the car heater. By the time she reached home, she had just begun to get warm.

She saw the white Cadillac in the driveway and smiled as she pulled in beside the large car. Trevor was sitting on the front porch playing with Clem, who had placed her empty food dish at his feet.

"Hi. Have you been here long?" she asked.

"No," he assured her as he stood to greet her. "Clem and I have been comparing hunger pangs."

Starr laughed as she bent to pick up Clem's bowl and unlock the door. "Well, if Clem's willing to share her dog chow with you, you're in luck."

Trevor's arms closed around her as he bent to bestow a kiss. A threatening growl from Clem stopped him. Eyeing her with a frown, he said, "Whose side are you on, anyway, girl? Remember who was responsible for the great cookie caper?"

Starr handed Trevor Clem's bowl as he followed her into the kitchen. Clem scurried after them, licking her chops in anticipation and rotating her bushy tail in excited circles.

"Here, you feed her and she's yours for life."

When Trevor returned from the porch, Starr had already started the salad. He lifted her hair and nuzzled the back of her neck. "Sprouts?"

At his touch the knife trembled in her unsteady hand. "Honestly, Trevor, I don't know what you have against sprouts," she complained, trying to keep her tone light.

His arms circled her waist. "They're stringy, tasteless, and ugly."

"Beauty is in the eye of the beholder," she informed him tartly.

"I agree," he whispered against her cheek and slowly turned her around to face his warm green eyes.

The knife dropped from her hand and fell to the floor with a noisy clatter.

"I hope I still have a foot left," Trevor said with a deadpan expression. "I'm afraid to look. You're going to finish me off one way or the other."

Starr slipped out of his embrace and opened the refrigerator. "You know what they say about too many cooks in the kitchen."

Trevor laughed as he picked up the paring knife. "You're just full of quotes and adages, aren't you?" There was a moment's silence and then he asked, "How did the meeting go tonight?"

Starr was glad her face was turned away from him. His sudden interjection about the council meeting stunned her. Was that why he had come tonight? To find out how she'd voted on his project?

"Fine," she answered in a noncommittal tone as she gripped the tomatoes she was holding. She carried the produce to the counter where Trevor was washing the knife she'd dropped. "We unanimously approved your development. You now have the green light to go full steam ahead."

"Great," he said with a broad smile that showed his gleaming white teeth. "Where's the dish towel?"

Puzzled, Starr opened the cabinet drawer and handed him a towel. Sometimes he was unfathomable, she thought as she watched him expertly cut the tomatoes into uniform wedges.

Together they prepared a large salad and Starr heated leftover soup.

"This won't be as elegant as halibut brochette, but I didn't know you were coming."

"Beggars can't be choosers," Trevor quipped with a grin.

Bowing her head, Starr uttered a simple prayer. "Bless this food, O Lord. Let it nourish our bodies and our spirits. We give thanks in your name. Amen."

"Amen," Trevor echoed as he buttered a bran muffin. "You amaze me, Starr."

She paused, the soup spoon midway to her

lips. "Why? Because I say grace? I don't believe in a public display of piety. My parents taught me to give thanks at all times—even if I had to do so silently."

"You amaze me because you're so rare. Outwardly, you look and act like the modern woman—smart, involved, dedicated. But deep inside is the most marvelous old-fashioned girl who still believes first and foremost in God and country. I've never met anyone quite like you, Starr." Admiration gleamed in his warm eyes.

"Ah, you mean my facade." A mischievous grin tugged at her lips.

"Ouch." Trevor threw up his hands in defeat. "You can't hold a guy responsible for what he says in the moonlight."

"I wouldn't if the guy had been complimentary."

His eyes softened as he reached over to grasp her hand. "I hope you weren't insulted by what I said. I admire you, ma'am. Even when you're bullheaded."

He ducked as she threw her napkin at him.

After dinner he helped her with the dishes, even though she protested it wasn't necessary. While she finished in the kitchen, Trevor laid the fire. When she joined him, he was staring into the flames.

"A penny for your thoughts," she said softly as she settled on the end of the sofa.

"I doubt if they're worth that much," he replied as he sat beside her. He smiled, but she had seen the frown that furrowed his forehead before he knew she was in the room. Starr wondered what was worrying him. The project? She had just told him it had been approved. Or were there matters of which she knew nothing? After all, she knew really very little about him.

The warmth of the fire lulled her senses and she nodded off to sleep. Unaccustomed to the late meal, she felt her limbs grow heavy with fatigue as she fought to keep her eyes open. It had been a long day. Her eyelids closed again and she drifted away into an uneasy slumber.

When Starr awakened, the fire had gone out and the room was cold. She glanced over at Trevor, who had also fallen asleep with his head resting on her shoulder. Unable to resist, she smoothed the tousled blond hair back from his forehead with gentle fingers. Trevor gave a deep sigh and snuggled closer.

On her rug in front of the fireplace, Clem was snoring with her usual loud symphony of snorts and gasps, punctuated occasionally by a loud yelp as she chased an errant cat in her dreams. *It must be after midnight,* Starr thought in alarm.

"Trevor," she whispered, shaking him gently. "Trevor, wake up. It's late."

Mumbling something totally unintelligible, he collapsed on her shoulder again. A few seconds later she could tell from the deep sound of his breathing that he had fallen asleep once more. Careful not to disturb him, Starr slid her shoulder from under his head and gently eased off the sofa.

When she returned from the bedroom with a pillow and a heavy quilt, he had slid further down on the sofa. Before covering him with the quilt, she carefully straightened his body as best she could and removed his shoes.

Before turning out the light, she took one last look at his peaceful face. His long dark lashes lay softly against his tanned cheeks. Gently, so gently, she traced the outline of his lips before bending to kiss him good-night.

"Take good care of him, Clem," she ordered as she headed for her own bed.

Clem's tail thumped in compliance as Starr turned out the light.

NINE
Illusions

Starr found Trevor's note under the sugar bowl the next morning.

"My dearest Starr," it began, "I want to thank you for a lovely evening. My apologies for zonking out on you like that. I've been putting in some long days at the site and working on my books at night. Thanks for tucking me in. I hope you gave me a good-night kiss. Love, Trevor. P.S. Clem and P.J. have been fed."

Starr held the note, staring at the firm, bold strokes of his handwriting. "My dearest Starr," she read the opening again. "Love, Trevor." Still clutching the note as though she would never let it go, she sat down with a heavy thud and finished her tea.

When Jan stopped by the store on her lunch hour, Starr was humming as she dusted shelves and discarded old stock.

"Well, aren't you Miss Polly Sunshine this morning?" Jan observed as she pulled up the bucket chair and collapsed with a tired sigh. She looked at Starr suspiciously. "If I didn't know better, I'd say you were in love."

Starr waved the feather duster at her. "Look who's talking. I never get to see you for more than five minutes since Bob Mason came to town."

Jan frowned at the mention of Bob's name. "I think that's going to change."

"What?" Starr exclaimed with an incredulous gasp. "Have you changed your mind about him?"

Jan laughed. "No way. I think he's the most wonderful man I've ever met."

"Oh," Starr groaned in mock agony, "here we go again."

"Well, he is," Jan insisted. "But I don't think I'm going to get to see much of him for a while because Trevor is pushing to complete as much of the construction as he can before bad weather sets in. Bob says Trevor will work every daylight hour to get the framing completed as soon as possible."

A sudden chill seized Starr. "You mean now that the project has the official go-ahead?"

"I guess," Jan confirmed with a vague look, unaware of the abrupt change in Starr's demeanor.

After Jan left, Starr gazed into space with a thoughtful expression. An uneasiness picked at her and she tried unsuccessfully to shove it away. Would she ever completely trust another man? Her father had always said she was a doubting Thomas, quick to judge, slow to forgive. She had trusted Kevin, never dreaming he would mete her such a blow.

The rest of the day dragged by slowly. A few of her regular customers stopped to buy large supplies of vitamin C tablets for their back-to-school children, hoping to eliminate the myriad colds that followed the opening week of school.

Friday was busy and Starr had little time to realize that Trevor hadn't called, nor had she seen him since Wednesday night after the council meeting.

As she drove home in a depressed mood Friday evening, she admitted to herself that she missed him. How was it possible to miss someone so much whom she'd known for so short a time?

"Well, I'm sure Jan's right," she told P.J. as she sautéed fresh mushrooms. "He's just busy with his job."

Although her body was tired, her mind refused to rest. Why doesn't he call? she asked herself for the hundredth time as she turned on her back and gazed at the ceiling. She fell asleep with that thought echoing in her troubled mind.

Saturday morning she met with thirty of her Youth For Christ group at the church to prepare for their afternoon bake sale. Reverend Hartford was already in the church office working on his Sunday sermon when she arrived at eight.

His blue eyes twinkled as she passed his door. "Good morning, Starr," he called as she slipped past him with a wave and went into the silent sanctuary of the church.

She sat in a deserted pew in the back, enjoying the darkened solitude. In the nearby fellowship hall she could hear her teenaged group's excited patter as they began unloading and sorting the donated baked items. Light streamed in through the stained-glass windows, scattering into a muted kaleidoscope of colors beside the silent organ. Yellow and white chrysanthemums decorated the altar. Pressing her warm forehead against the pew in front of her, Starr began to pray.

"Help me, Lord," she whispered. "I'm so filled with doubt about everything and everyone including myself."

"Starr? Is anything wrong? Can I help?"

Startled, she felt Reverend Hartford's hand on her shoulder. "No," she said quickly. "I just came in here to think."

He sat down beside her in the pew. "It's a good place for that. I come in here quite a bit myself to think and to talk to my Boss." He chuckled as his warm blue eyes studied her troubled face. "Is the YFC group too much for you? I know how busy you are with your shop and the council. I know they can be a handful— all that energy. But they think so much of you—"

"Oh, no," she reassured him. "I love my kids. You know, we raised enough money to re-plant that whole hill that the mining company left bare after they shut down their operations. They're a great bunch of workers," she said with admiration.

"They've got a great advisor," Reverend Hartford said. He patted her arm in a comforting gesture. "Well, if you're sure there's nothing I can do—"

"No. I'd better get over to the hall to be sure they haven't eaten all the goodies before we get a chance to sell them this afternoon."

Chuckling, the reverend headed back to his small office.

When Starr arrived, the fellowship hall was an arena of busy activity. Sometimes she was so proud of her YFC group that she thought they could have gotten along fine without any supervision. As she opened the door, Joe Fielding chose that moment to swat Fred Wilson, and she amended her previous thought to "most of the time."

"OK, guys, where are we in this mess?"

Joe and Fred immediately snapped to attention. Starr spent a few minutes supervising the setting up of the tables and appointing cashiers. Joe cast an appreciative glance as Laura Ames walked by carrying a large cake.

He leaned over and whispered in Starr's ear. "Can you put me at the same table with Laura?"

"Only if you promise to behave."

Fred chortled at that remote possibility and Laura turned around with a questioning look in her wide brown eyes.

"You dummy," Joe fumed at him. "Now look what you've done."

"Knock it off, you two," Starr ordered. "And start carrying this stuff outside."

By three that afternoon the baked goods had dwindled to nearly nothing. Being around the group lifted Starr's depressed mood and she found herself laughing at their high-spirited pranks. Frequently they seemed to forget that she was supposed to be the supervisor, as they included her in their conversations and plans. Her initial fears of not being able to communicate effectively with them had long ago dissipated.

"OK, group," she told them a little after four, "I think we can start putting all this stuff back in the hall. There's nothing left but a couple of plates of cookies and one cake."

Joe snickered. "You know whose cake that is, don't you, Starr?"

"Yes, I do," she said. "But we can't complain if Mrs. Tolford puts too much baking powder in everything. We should be grateful that she wants to help." Starr was having a hard time keeping a straight face. Everyone in town knew what poor Mrs. Tolford's cakes looked like and they were never bought until last.

"As long as we don't have to eat it," Fred snickered.

"I should make you two buy it," Starr chastised with as stern an expression as she could muster.

"Ah, Starr. Have a heart," Joe whined.

"Problem, Starr?"

Reverend Hartford had quietly joined the group.

"No problem, Reverend," she assured him. "Joe and Fred were just arguing about who was going to buy the last cake."

"Really?" the reverend commented with a faint lift of his eyebrow. He peeked at the remaining cake. "I imagine it would make Mrs. Tolford very happy to know her baking skills were in such demand."

Laura was unable to stifle a laugh at his remark and the whole group was soon laughing.

"Well," Reverend Hartford said as he pulled out his billfold, "how much is it? I believe I've bought every cake the poor dear has baked for the last ten years."

"Half price, Reverend," Starr told him. "And we'll throw in the cookies as a bonus."

After her group had cleaned up the hall, carried out the garbage, and washed and dried the big electric coffee pot, Starr let them go. "Great job, all of you," she called as the last of the teenagers filed out the door.

Alone in the hall, she counted out the crumpled dollar bills and stacked the coins in neat little piles. The YFC funds had been completely depleted for their replanting project. Now, with Christmas just a few months away, they would have to double their efforts to reach the goal of a basket for every senior citizen in the community. Starr knew somehow they would do it. They were great kids and she was unbelievably proud of them.

A fleeting sadness was reflected in her wide blue eyes as she stared into the flower garden outside the church hall. Would she ever have children of her own to love and nurture? Trevor had said she would make a wonderful mother. She pushed thoughts of Trevor from her mind. She was foolish for thinking of him as much as she did. After all, he wouldn't be in Springfield forever. When the housing project was completed, he would be returning to California.

She zipped the bank bag and carried it into Reverend Hartford's office. Anna Dickey, his part-time secretary, looked up over her reading glasses as the door opened.

"How did the sale go, Starr? Looked like quite a crowd out there when I came in to work."

"Fine," Starr said as she handed the bag to her. "We sold everything."

"Everything?" Anna asked as her dark eyes twinkled in amusement.

"Yep. Sold the last batch at a discount to Reverend Hartford."

"The poor man," Anna empathized. "I saw him leaving a few minutes ago with Mrs. Tolford's cake."

Starr laughed. "He's a sweetheart. He can't bear to see her feelings hurt."

The phone rang, and as Anna picked it up, she said, "See you in church tomorrow, dear."

Starr nodded and left for home. She spent Saturday night in front of the fireplace alternately reading and thinking. Occasionally she glanced at the silent phone as she strove to discard the doubts that plagued her. Drowsy from the heat, she fell asleep, until Clem's whining awakened her.

Staggering to the door, she stood waiting for Clem to attend to the call of nature. The bright stars looked cold and remote in the black sky. Shivering, she peered into the darkness. "Hurry up, Clem. I'm freezing."

By the time she retired to bed she was fully

awake. P.J.'s purring beside her was comforting as she stared wide-eyed into the dark room. "We'll manage, won't we, sweetheart?" she asked as she stroked the long-haired cat.

After church Sunday she drove to Peace Gardens. Carrying some of the yellow chrysanthemums from the altar, she walked slowly between the rows of neatly spaced tombstones until she came to the last two stones at the rear of the cemetery. Kneeling on the grass, she carefully placed the flowers around the granite stones. Tears brimmed in her sad blue eyes as she traced the engravings with her fingers. John Adams Monroe. Rebecca Tyler Monroe. Beloved husband. Beloved wife.

"Hi, Mom. Hi, Dad," she whispered. "I brought you some flowers. I knew you'd like them, Mom. They're yellow."

The tears coursed freely down her cheeks. Her mother had loved yellow roses. They were the pride of her garden. As often as possible she brought a single yellow rose from her mother's garden and left it beside the cold, gray stone.

For a few more minutes Starr remained by the graves, listening to the chatter of the squirrels in the nearby oak trees. Sunlight filtered through the leaves and fell in a dappled pattern of golden light on the twin stones. How she missed them both, she thought as she rose from the grass and brushed her skirt. She walked slowly toward the car, almost reluctant to leave the tranquillity of the surroundings. Peace Gardens. The place was well named.

Monday morning brought cloudy skies that

persisted until Wednesday. Standing at the window of the store, Starr gazed out at the bleak day. Trevor still had not called or stopped to see her. Several times she had thought about calling him, but each time she picked up the phone, pride held her back. Had it been only a week since he'd spent the night on her couch? It seemed more like a year.

On her way to the council meeting that night she headed the small car toward the construction site. Even before she pulled onto Turkey Knob, she could hear the machinery and men at work. Although it was nearly dark, the site was still a melee of activity. She watched for a few minutes before hurrying on to the courthouse.

The meeting was a routine one. The motion was carried to install new stop signs at Main and Elm Streets. The cost of a traffic signal was too prohibitive even to consider. Mayor Russell was pleased to report that several local men had been hired for the Hall housing project. Starr listened to the report with mixed emotions. The members approved several small recommendations by the mayor before adjourning.

After the meeting, Starr was standing by the coffee machine in the hallway when Burton joined her.

"Hello, gorgeous. You're not drinking this poison, are you?" he asked as he inserted two quarters and waited for the Styrofoam cup to drop down.

"What? Oh, no," she hastened to assure him. "Just standing here thinking."

"The mayor sure is pleased with his bosom buddy from California," Burton said as he stirred his coffee.

"What do you mean?" Burton was never closemouthed when he knew of some gossip that could be spread.

"Aren't you the innocent one? Didn't Trevor Hall wine and dine you like he did the rest of us to get your vote? Granted, we all didn't get the royal treatment the mayor did, but—"

"Wine and dine?" Starr interrupted.

"Sure. He spent time with everyone on the council. I can't believe you were neglected."

An icy spiral moved upward in Starr's chest. Her intense distrust of men returned more forcefully than ever. He had used her to get the green light for his precious project.

"Why did you vote for him if you felt you were being coerced?"

"I'm not stupid, Starr. I'd like to get reelected to the council. I know what that project's going to do for this town. I would have voted for him anyway. But you," he paused and looked at her curiously, "surprised me. I didn't think you'd ever vote for that development."

Starr faltered under his gaze and leaned against the coffee machine. Men, she thought in disgust.

"Starr, are you all right?"

From somewhere in the blind fog that covered her mind, she could hear his anxious voice. "I'm fine, Burt," she murmured as she staggered down the hall. "Just wonderful."

She stood at the door of the courthouse look-ing up and down the street before venturing out. Her little yellow car looked lonely under the street lamp. Burton's words kept echoing in her mind as she ran toward the car. A sharp sob caught in her throat. Once again she had been a fool.

When the phone rang, she was getting ready for bed.

"Hi, beautiful. How are you?"

Starr froze at the sound of his voice. As much as she disliked him at the moment, her heart skipped strangely as she listened to him.

"Starr, are you all right?"

"I'm OK," she finally answered.

"I'm awfully sorry I haven't called or been able to see you. I had to fly to New York to get some supplies and we've been working around the clock since I got back."

She remained silent.

"Starr, what's wrong?"

"Wrong?" she whispered as she looked out the bedroom window at the rising moon. "Nothing is wrong. You don't have to continue your act now, Trevor. The project is safe. You can quit romancing the little country bumpkin."

"What are you talking about?" A hint of anger had crept into his voice along with the confusion.

She sat on the edge of the bed, holding the phone tightly clenched in her hand. "You know, Trevor, that I was the only one on the council who was really against the project. It wouldn't have been necessary to ingratiate yourself so thoroughly with the other members. We both know this whole thing has been an act. You wanted only one thing from me—and that was my vote."

She waited for him to deny it. Oh, how she wanted to hear him say it wasn't true. To hear him say he had really fallen in love with her.

"Is that what you think I did?" His warm voice had turned to ice. "Told you I loved you in exchange for a vote?"

"Weren't you concerned about how I voted?"

"Yes," he admitted.

His coolness ruffled her already rising temper. "It's too bad, Trevor, that there aren't any other women on the council. With your line you wouldn't have had any trouble winning them all over."

"Are you trying to say you think I'm guilty of emotional bribery? Or maybe you're calling me worse. Since your opinion of me is obviously so low—"

"Didn't you spend time with the mayor and the rest of the council to influence their votes? And I thought I was so special because—" she broke off, unable to finish.

"It was the mayor's idea for me to get acquainted with everyone on the council. To explain my project."

Starr felt sick. He wouldn't even admit the truth about the situation. He had to put the blame on someone else.

"Was it the mayor's idea to take me to the construction site in the moonlight?"

There was a long silence.

"No," he said in a tightly controlled voice. "That was my idea."

Tears blinded Starr. "Well, don't waste any more of your wonderful ideas or time on me, Trevor," she blurted out angrily as she slammed down the phone.

Five minutes later when the phone rang again she ignored it. She buried her head in the pillow and cried until there were no more tears left. He had admitted that he'd used her. Had he no conscience? And he called himself a Christian! No wonder he said it was hard being a good businessman and a good Christian at the same time. For Trevor, business evidently came first—in every aspect of his life.

For a long time Starr lay awake, watching the moon glide and skirt the summer sky. A gentle breeze billowed the sheer curtains as she wrestled with the horrible emptiness that threatened to consume her. She should have known better than to have trusted him. Once a fool, always a fool.

It wasn't the end of the world, she reassured herself as she pressed her warm face to her damp pillow.

It just seemed to be.

TEN
Life
Goes On

Cautiously, autumn was approaching. The nights were turning cooler and early morning frosts were not at all unusual.

Starr stood at the kitchen window watching the first rays of sunshine strike the patches of white frost. As far as she could see, the green meadow was aglow with the sparkle of nature's diamonds, which yielded their luster only after the warm rays had evaporated them.

She sighed and stirred her tea with absent-minded disinterest. How could she have been so wrong about Trevor? It was still hard to believe that she had meant no more to him than a vote, but she had heard it from his own lips. And worse, he had offered no apologies for his immoral behavior.

"Evidently the Lord wants me to learn something from this experience or it would never have happened," she remarked to Clem, who was curled up in front of the door.

Opening one eye, Clem waited for her to continue.

"Wine and dine," Starr muttered as she dumped the rest of her tea down the drain. Burton's words had cut through her like a razor. And she had been foolish enough to think she was special to Trevor. She felt used, manipulated, and yes, angry. Unfortunately, the brunt of her anger was directed toward herself rather than Trevor.

"I'll never learn, I guess," she murmured as she slipped on her sweater and let Clem outside onto the porch.

As she drove slowly to the store, she kept her eyes on the road, ignoring the first touches of brilliant fall coloring that lined both sides of the highway.

A steady stream of customers kept her busy all morning. Shortly before noon, Jan called to ask her to lunch.

"I don't think so," she hedged. "I've been busy all morning and there's a lot of stock to be unpacked and put on the shelves."

"Are you all right? You sound funny." Jan had sensed that something was wrong.

"Sure. I'm fine," Starr insisted with a forced brightness. "I'm just not hungry. I'll talk to you later."

Before Jan could further question her, she quickly hung up the telephone. The last thing she wanted was to talk to Jan or anyone else

148

about how foolish and gullible she'd been.

Still, every time the bell chimed over the door, she looked up in apprehension, half expecting to see Trevor's tall body outlined in the doorway.

"Come on, Starr, get with it," she chastised herself as she ripped open a case of vitamins with a vengeance that severed the lid from the box. She let out a sharp cry of pain as her nail tore into the quick.

"Starr, are you all right?"

Through tears of anger she saw Mary Lou Williams eyeing her with a look of concern.

"Just ripped half of my nail off. Excuse me a minute, Mary Lou."

She ran to the back room and plunged her finger under the cold water to stop the bleeding. Splashing her cheeks with the cold water, she tried to compose herself before returning to the front of the store.

"What are you doing here at this time of day, Mary Lou? School's not out yet, is it?" She smiled at the tall, auburn-haired girl as she wrapped a bandage around her throbbing finger.

"No, I left at lunch." At Starr's raised eyebrow, she hastened to explain. "I have study hall this period. I told Miss Weaver you wanted to see me about YFC and she gave me permission to come.

"Yes, I do want to see you, Mary Lou. Please sit down."

Starr turned the sign on the door to read "Closed" and locked the door.

Mary Lou perched nervously on the edge of

the plastic chair and gazed around the interior of the small store, all the while deliberately avoiding Starr's eyes.

Leaning against the counter, Starr wondered how to begin. At this particular time she certainly didn't feel qualified to be dispensing advice about male-female relationships, but....

"Mary Lou," she said softly, trying to cushion her accusation, "I've missed you at our YFC meetings. You used to be one of our most regular members."

A pink flush climbed slowly up from Mary Lou's neck until it reached her cheeks, where it deepened to a brilliant scarlet and disappeared into her dark auburn hair.

"I've been busy," she murmured, her eyes downcast as she pretended to study the pattern in the tile flooring.

Starr remained silent for a moment as she studied the unhappy girl. If she accused her of what she knew to be true, she would immediately alienate Mary Lou and destroy any hope of communicating with her.

"Your mother called last week because she thought you were at the meeting."

The girl looked up at her with sudden fright mirrored in her gray eyes.

"I didn't tell her that you hadn't been there at all."

Mary Lou exhaled a sigh of relief.

"But," Starr said, her face growing stern, "I won't do it again, Mary Lou. You've been using the group and me to give you an alibi to see Don Hoover, haven't you?"

The gray eyes grew defiant.

"Mary Lou, you can't keep something like this quiet in a small town. Your parents are going to find out sooner or later and then they'll be hurt because you've lied to them."

"They don't understand," Mary Lou blurted out as she burst into tears. "Don and I want to get married. It's their fault that we have to sneak around."

Starr handed her a box of tissues and waited for the tears to abate before she continued.

"Mary Lou, you're only sixteen. Don't you think you owe it to yourself to finish your education? If you don't get that diploma now, you may never do it. If you and Don really love each other, you'll wait. If you run off and get married, think of the precious memories that'll never be yours. You'll miss graduation, your senior activities, all those things you should have to cherish forever. And you'll always feel guilty for hurting your folks."

Mary Lou looked at her in alarm.

"Oh, I know you've been planning to elope with Don. The whole town does. That's another memory you'll miss. Instead of a beautiful church wedding, you'll be all alone without any friends to celebrate one of the most important days of your life."

Starr seated herself in the other chair and grasped Mary Lou's hand.

"Wait until you're older, Mary Lou. Then, if you still feel the same, perhaps it'll be easier to convince your folks that you're doing the right thing."

A shadow of fear flickered in the deep gray eyes. "It's a long time until graduation. Don might find someone else."

We're all alike! Starr's mind screamed. Age doesn't matter. We're always afraid of losing someone's love.

"Then you don't have a very strong basis for marriage, do you? Give it some time, Mary Lou. Your folks have loved and trusted you all these years. Don't make them wrong in their judgment."

"I don't know—"

"I wouldn't worry about losing Don. From what I hear he's so busy running that farm for his dad that he rarely gets away from it."

"That's true," Mary Lou agreed. "I hardly ever get to see him."

Starr glanced at her watch. "You'd better get back to school."

At the door she hugged the younger girl. "Just promise me that you'll think over what I told you. OK?"

"I will, Starr. And thanks for taking the time to talk to me."

Starr shut the door, leaving the "Closed" sign turned out and headed for the back room to make a cup of peppermint tea. A vague ache over her right temple warned her that a headache was forthcoming.

"Life's a headache," she muttered as she scowled at the screaming teakettle. She wasn't sure that anything she'd said had made an impression on Mary Lou, but she'd tried. When you're sixteen and have just discovered the wonders of love. . . . Starr nearly choked on her tea. The wonders of love would be more aptly called the horrors of love.

With a resigned sigh, she finished the tea and opened the store. Despite it all, life went on and the bills had to be paid.

Through the week Starr continued to avoid Jan, although she missed her and the children with an intensity that was surprising. For the first time she didn't want to confide in Jan about Trevor. Wondering if she was really foolish, she unplugged the telephone at home, reasoning that if people wanted to get in touch with her, they could do so at the store. But at best, her lack of communication only made the long nights longer.

As the days crept by on leaden feet, she found herself talking to P.J. and Clem with an alarming regularity.

"Don't fall for any green-eyed blonds, Clem. They'll only be after your doggie treats." She affectionately rubbed the cold nose and was rewarded with a sloppy kiss on the chin.

Mayor Russell was out of town for a couple of weeks, so he canceled the council meetings, for which Starr was secretly relieved. The hiatus would give her time to pull herself together before facing Burton's prying eyes again.

Mary Lou attended the next YFC meeting and a tiny spark of happiness ignited in Starr's heart.

With Mary Lou back in the fold, she felt like a good shepherd. A warm rush of pleasure welled up in her. Her lost sheep had come home.

As she listened to the high-spirited laughter of the group, Starr turned away suddenly to hide her brimming tears.

She had never felt so alone in her whole life.

ELEVEN
Wedding Bells

Starr dragged through the next few days in a mental stupor. A deep depression had taken hold of her and she found it impossible to shake it off. At night she lay awake praying, until she fell asleep, her face wet with tears. Her appetite waned until she finally gave up all pretense of eating. She brewed countless cups of tea and sat staring at them until they were too cold to drink.

The days slowly turned to weeks, and still she had heard nothing from Trevor. Although a sense of guilt nagged at her, she continued to avoid Jan. On a glorious, crisp Sunday morning she slid into the last pew of the church and scanned the rows, looking for a familiar blond head. Well, she thought as she stood and opened her hymnbook, why did I think he'd be in church? His goal has already been accomplished. Why bother putting up a good front now?

Realizing how bitter her thoughts had become, she stopped singing and lowered the book. An old maid. That's what she'd be. Men were not to be trusted. From now on her heart would be closed. Oh, she would love animals and children—the world in general. But never, absolutely never, would she believe another man when he spoke of love.

Turning her damp eyes to the stained-glass windows where the sun was streaming through in brilliant hues, she prayed fervently as the organ softly played "What a Friend We Have in Jesus." She bit her lip as she fought back the tears. It wouldn't look good to see an upstanding member of the community, a city council member, crying in church.

As Reverend Hartford spoke the final words of the blessing, Starr slipped quickly from her seat and hurried out the side door. Normally she left church with a lighter heart, but today she walked with her shoulders drooped as if the weight of the world rested there.

"Starr!"

Reluctantly she paused at her car as she heard her name called.

"Jan," she cried as they fell into each other's arms. She'd missed her old friend more than she realized.

Melissa and Frank were scrubbed and shining, dressed in their Sunday best. Frank looked uncomfortable as he fidgeted in his navy blue suit.

"I didn't see you in church," Starr said as she straightened Melissa's hairbow.

Jan flashed a guilty smile. "I was there. I promised Bob I'd start going to church and taking the kids to Sunday school. He was a little upset with me when he found out I rarely took them."

Starr suppressed a frown. For the last couple of years she had tried unsuccessfully to get Jan to take Frank and Melissa to church. Now Bob had managed to accomplish it within a matter of weeks. A slight irritation nagged her. She had never coerced Jan. Perhaps she should have.

The congregation was moving steadily out the front door and down the steps of the little church. Starr cast a nervous glance at the oncoming rush of people. She just wasn't in the mood to talk to anyone today.

Jan grasped her hand. "Come to dinner. Do you have any plans?"

Starr hesitated. If Bob was going to be there, she'd feel like a fifth wheel. "I don't know, Jan. Is Bob coming? I don't want to intrude." She felt as though she'd lost her best friend on top of everything else.

Jan's big brown eyes grew wide with surprise. "Bob? I thought you knew he and Trevor left for California a few days ago."

The earth slowly crumbled around Starr. "No, I didn't know," she murmured, aware that Jan was staring at her with a puzzled expression.

Jan continued to gaze at her in confusion.

"Trevor and I had a violent argument a few weeks ago," she confessed finally, venturing only the barest outline of the facts. She had no desire to relive that horrible episode in any manner.

The warm breeze lifted her dark hair and blew it in front of her eyes, hiding the tears that rose to her sad blue eyes at the mention of Trevor's name.

"Well, come to dinner. I haven't seen you in weeks. The kids will be good. I promise."

Starr laughed and promised she would be there a little after six.

At home, she sat in the swing on the front porch with an untouched egg salad sandwich and a glass of iced tea beside her. As a neighbor drove by and honked his horn, she lifted a hand in greeting. A deep ache was welling inside her. All the way home she had kept telling herself it didn't matter that he had gone without even saying good-bye. Why should he? There was no longer any need to pretend.

Clem joined her on the porch, looking for a cool place to nap. The capricious autumn weather had turned warm again and the big dog was uncomfortable.

Starr looked wistfully at her companion. "What do you think of men, Clem?"

The fluffy tail pounded happily on the wooden floor.

"Oh, you're a sucker, too, huh?"

Clem opened her sleepy brown eyes for a moment to gaze at her unhappy mistress. She yawned and cuddled up for her afternoon nap.

"You never have to worry about a broken heart, do you, girl?"

Clem's tail beat in agreement.

"You liked him, too, didn't you?" Starr whispered as she reached down to scratch the floppy ears and was rewarded with a wet, sloppy kiss on the hand.

How trusting and loving she was, Starr thought as she petted the big dog. If only humans could trust and love each other with that same kind of blind faith. But humans became wary after each hurt and grew more guarded in their relationships. The walls grew higher and higher until all trust was gone.

"Oh, Trevor," she sobbed as she gazed out across the dark green mountains. "Why did it have to turn out this way?"

For a long time Starr sat staring out across the distant hills, thinking about Trevor being in California. A lump rose in her throat and she gave the egg salad sandwich to Clem, who downed it in a gulp.

"I'm going to have to put you on a diet," she threatened as she hugged Clem's bulging sides.

Carrying date-nut cookies and a green bean casserole, she rang Jan's doorbell a little after six.

Melissa and Frank squealed in delight as they hugged her repeatedly, but Jan seemed a little nervous as she greeted Starr.

When the enthusiastic welcoming from the children had abated, she helped Jan set the table. Jan chattered incessantly about nothing, which wasn't like her at all.

Starr smoothed a small wrinkle in the embroidered tablecloth. "OK, Jan, what is it?"

"What do you mean?" she said a bit too brightly as she avoided looking at Starr.

Starr waited, her arms crossed.

Sighing, Jan sat down on the kitchen chair and fidgeted with a fork. "I was sort of waiting for the right opportunity to tell you this. You've been like a sister to me since Frank died and I want your approval of what I'm planning to do."

Starr let out a long sigh of relief. "I've never known you to do anything dishonest or immoral, so shoot. It can't be that bad, Jan."

Jan gave a weak smile, took a deep breath, and blurted, "Bob and I are going to be married as soon as he and Trevor return from California. He asked me last week."

"Married!" Starr exclaimed as she stared at Jan in shock. "I knew you were serious, but—" She lapsed into a stunned silence.

"Oh, Starr," Jan said as she grabbed her hand in a desperate appeal. "I love him so much. When Frank died, I thought my life was over. I was so sure I'd never love anyone else again." She paused to regain her composure.

"I'm happy for you," Starr managed to say quietly. It was wonderful that things were working out for Jan and Bob. She thought of Trevor and immediately pushed away the image of those haunting green eyes.

"He loves the children," Jan continued in a dreamy voice, "and that's very important to me. Not every man would be happy taking on the responsibilities of a ready-made family, but Bob is crazy about Frank and Melissa."

Starr nodded. She had observed the look on Bob's face when he was playing with Jan's children, and they loved and accepted him already as a father. She squeezed Jan's hand and smiled at her through tear-filled eyes. "I'm really pleased, Jan. It's just that it's so sudden. I guess I wasn't prepared to hear you say marriage."

Jan had already told the children that Bob would be their new daddy soon, and they talked about it with great excitement throughout the dinner. Listening politely, Starr hoped she was smiling at the right time and saying the right words in response to their enthusiasm. Her mind was several miles away—a few thousand to be exact.

Melissa's tug on her arm brought her back to reality. "Are you going to marry Uncle Trevor?" she asked with childlike innocence.

Starr gasped at the unexpected question. A stab of pain twisted in her chest. "No," she assured Melissa as the child's face clouded with disappointment. She gathered Melissa in her arms as she tried to explain.

"Uncle Trevor and I don't get along too well."

Jan began to clear the table. "Melissa, why don't you and Frank go outside and play so Aunt Starr and I can talk?"

They scampered from the kitchen and a few seconds later the door banged after them. Starr busied herself with scraping the dishes. Uncle Trevor. He certainly had wasted no time ingratiating himself with Frank and Melissa!

Assured that the children were out of earshot, Jan prompted Starr. "What's this with you and Trevor? You two need to talk."

"I don't want to discuss Trevor, if you don't mind, Jan." With a look of fierce determination, Starr turned away from her friend's troubled eyes.

"Oh, Starr, I don't know what's wrong, but you can't let this happen between you two. I talked to Bob this afternoon and he said Trevor is so hurt over the situation he won't even talk about it. Can't it be settled?"

"I will never forgive him for using me to gain his own ends."

Jan plunged the plate into the hot, sudsy water and rubbed vigorously with the sponge. "I can't imagine Trevor using anyone—most of all, you, Starr. The man's crazy about you. I've watched him look at you. I know when a man's in love."

"Love," Starr said in disgust. "He doesn't know the meaning of that word any more than he does the meaning of being Christian." A plate fell from her hand and broke on the tiled floor.

"It's all right, honey," Jan assured her as she swept up the pieces and dropped them into the wastebasket. "The kids have broken so many pieces already. Let's sit on the porch. I'll finish the dishes later."

They sat in the glider on the front porch watching the children play hopscotch on the sidewalk. The sounds of their laughter floated happily on the evening air and Starr felt her heart lighten as she watched them.

"Starr, I did invite you here tonight for a reason. I have a favor to ask."

"Since when do you have to invite me to dinner to ask a favor?" Her blue eyes widened.

"I know it's not much notice," Jan continued, "but I want you to be my maid of honor."

"I'm delighted," Starr assured her with a forced smile. "And honored."

"You know," Jan said softly as though trying to cushion the blow, "Trevor will be Bob's best man."

For a long moment Starr remained absolutely motionless. "If you don't think our dislike of each other will ruin your wedding, I'd still be happy to be your maid of honor."

Shedding tears of happiness, they hugged each other as Frank and Melissa came running to see what was wrong.

I am happy for her, Starr thought as she drove home. Jan deserved someone like Bob. Although she had to admit that the thought of standing along with Trevor throughout the ceremony made her shiver in apprehension. Determined not to disappoint Jan, she decided to grin and bear it. She would smile and be charming if it killed her. When the wedding was over, she'd go home and cry for a month.

As she helped Jan make preparations for the

wedding, the days seemed to move much too quickly. Starr wondered if Jan might not have been too impulsive about setting a date such a short time away. Every evening she breathed a sigh of relief if she was able to scratch at least one or two items from her long list of things yet to be done. Jan talked to Bob in California every day, but Trevor was never mentioned, for which Starr was grateful. He was out of her life, and the less she knew about him the better off she was. Or so she told herself, as the day of the wedding grew closer.

Starr sat on the plush velvet sofa in the bridal salon of Goodman's Department Store waiting for Jan to model one of the dresses she had selected. They had been in every department store, boutique, and mall within a hundred-mile radius of Springfield, and Starr was tired. Jan must have tried on every suitable dress in her size in every store—and hadn't liked any of them.

Leafing through a bridal magazine, Starr found herself thinking about the exquisite gown she'd worn as she stood at the altar waiting for Kevin. Well, she'd never have to worry about that again. Once was more than enough. The Salvation Army had been the happy recipient of that dress, and she still hated looking at wedding apparel.

"Starr?"

Choking back a sob, she looked up as Jan twirled in front of her in a street-length dress of pale mint green.

"Oh, Jan, it's perfect," she whispered.

The white-haired clerk also smiled her approval as she and Starr stared in mutual awe at Jan's transformation in the satin creation.

"You look radiant," Starr said as the magazine slipped from her fingers. As much as she loved Jan, a small tinge of jealousy stung her for a passing moment.

"Do you really like it?" Jan asked as she beamed at her reflection in the mirrors.

"Jan," Starr assured her in a dry tone, "even if we looked at another fifty dresses, we wouldn't find one more perfect."

Starr soon discovered that Jan's dress was just the beginning. Ensembles still had to be purchased for Frank and Melissa. And there was her own dress—which she refused to let Jan buy.

"We should have started two months ago," Starr grumbled as they trudged into the East Town Mall.

Pushing her through the door, Jan said, "I didn't know two months ago, dear."

Starr's face grew serious as she studied her friend's glowing eyes. "Are you sure about Bob, Jan? It is so sudden and—"

"No doubts, Starr," Jan said firmly. "Now let's find a dress for you."

It was after ten when they returned to Jan's small house. Laden with packages and giggling like school girls, they fell exhausted onto the couch.

"The children are asleep," Mrs. Ludlow informed them as she held a warning finger to her lips.

"I'm sorry we're so late," Jan apologized as she rummaged through her purse for the babysitting money. "The time just got away from us, I guess."

"It's quite all right, Mrs. Stevens."

Starr reluctantly pushed her tired body up from the couch. "I'll be glad to take you home, Mrs. Ludlow." In reality, she felt if she moved another step it would kill her.

"It's only a few blocks, Starr. I don't mind walking." She picked up her knitting and slipped into a heavy sweater.

Jan waited until she was out of sight before turning off the outside light.

"She's a jewel," she remarked with a tired sigh as she plopped down on the couch beside Starr.

"A nice lady," Starr agreed, resting her aching feet on the coffee table. "Did we miss any stores in that shopping center?"

"I don't think so! But at least we got nearly everything."

"What do you mean **nearly** everything?" Starr groaned. "I'm not going shopping with you again. It'll take me a year to pay off all this stuff you talked me into buying!"

"You haven't bought anything for yourself in years, Starr Monroe. It was a good chance to make you buy some nice new clothes."

"I'll bet you're getting married just so I have to buy new clothes."

That remark started them on a new round of giggling.

"Shh," Jan cautioned, "we'll have the little ones up if we aren't quiet."

The phone rang and Jan rushed to answer it with an expectant glow in her brown eyes. Slipping on her shoes, Starr began separating their purchases. Not wanting to eavesdrop on the conversation, she carried her things to the car. When she had finished, she waited in the kitchen for Jan.

"That was Bob," she said, her eyes aglow with a brilliant luster.

"I never would have guessed."

"They'll arrive tomorrow. The wedding's on for Sunday."

Starr's stomach fluttered at Jan's news, even though it was expected. Suddenly she didn't feel so brave about facing Trevor at the wedding. One look at Jan's happy face and she knew it was too late to back out now.

She picked up her purse and the last two packages. "I'd better go."

At the door she glanced back at Jan and shook her head. She was in another world. Steady, reliable, feet-on-the-ground-at-all-times Jan was on cloud nine.

Starr awakened the next morning with a tight feeling in her chest. She was slightly nauseated. Then she remembered it was Saturday and tomorrow was the wedding. She had decided to close the store for the day. There was still a lot to be done before the wedding tomorrow afternoon. With Bob arriving today she doubted that Jan would be in any condition to remember everything she should. Lying in bed, she ran over the plans for the reception in her head. She had planned on sleeping in, but her active mind refused to let her enjoy that luxury.

Starr spent the morning on the phone double-checking the preparations and making last-minute arrangements. Too nervous to eat any lunch, she stood at the counter and drank a glass of milk to calm her nerves. Her stomach continued to grind in anxiety as she fought back the fear of facing Trevor. She was being silly, she told herself. They were civilized people. But she couldn't forget the anger in his voice the last time they had spoken to each other.

She washed her hair and immersed herself in a long bubble bath before changing into a pair of white slacks and a turquoise silk blouse she had bought on her buying spree. The white slacks accentuated her long slim legs, and the deep blue of the blouse made her eyes sparkle. Jan was right. She did feel better in her new clothes. The caress of the silk blouse against her skin was exquisite.

When she arrived at the church for the rehearsal, her palms were damp with perspiration. Jan, Bob, and the children were waiting with Reverend Hartford in his office. Starr glanced around the room nervously.

"Trevor can't make it to the rehearsal," Jan informed her as the reverend began issuing instructions. "He's trying to catch up on some book work."

"Oh," Starr replied, not sure whether she was disappointed or relieved.

They ran through the ceremony a couple of times. Frank and Melissa were a little unsure of the whole situation. Tears brimmed in Starr's eyes as she watched Jan and Bob holding hands and gazing into each other's eyes. **Always a bridesmaid, never a bride**, she thought as she went through her paces for the third time.

After the rehearsal, they went to the café on Main Street. Jan was sentimental about the small restaurant because it was where she and Bob had met such a short time ago. The children ordered hamburgers and fries. For once Starr remained silent about their choice of food.

Looking at Bob's warm, friendly face, she longed to ask him about Trevor, but choked back the useless inquiry. What did it matter? Frowning, Starr tried to assimilate the information about Trevor's being hurt by her remarks. After all, it was she who had suffered. Why should he be hurt?

She stole a quick glance at Bob as he bent close to Jan to hear what she was saying over Frank's chatter. As manipulative and charming as Trevor was, he'd have no problem in fooling someone nice like Bob who believed the best of everyone. He'd fooled **her**, and she usually didn't trust men at all.

"Starr, why the frown?"

Bob's soft inquiry snapped her back to reality. "I didn't realize I was frowning," she murmured.

Although she was glad that Millie chose that moment to bring their orders, she gazed at the food placed before her with revulsion. She picked up the fork and pushed the overdone vegetables around on the plate as she made a listless attempt at eating. She was worse than the children.

Bob had made the children bow their heads and give thanks before eating.

A warm feeling enveloped Starr as she smiled at Bob. At least some good had resulted from Trevor's coming to their little town. Bob would be there during the years the children were growing up, to help Jan guide them. He would be a good father. Tears sprang to her eyes and she dabbed at them.

"Starr, are you crying?"

Jan's warm brown eyes were filled with concern.

"No. I have something in my eye. That's all."

Knowing better, Bob gave her a tender smile of understanding.

She became aware of the tall figure standing beside her and knew without looking up who it was.

"Trevor," Jan exclaimed in delight, "you were able to make it after all!"

Starr had turned to ice at the mention of his name. She kept her attention on her plate as he offered his greetings to everyone at the table.

"Miss Monroe," he said coldly, "if you would be so kind as to move over, I'll join the party."

When she glanced up to meet his cold green eyes, she was glad that the children's chatter covered her embarrassment to some extent. She shivered at the reproach mirrored in his icy gaze.

As he talked to Jan and Bob, Starr stole quick glances at him from under her dark eyelashes. He looked thinner and his hair was a little longer. Worry seemed to be etched on his haggard face.

The dark green silk shirt he wore deepened his blond coloring, and Starr found it almost impossible to tear her eyes away from him. It seemed as if all the appetite she lacked for food was directed toward him. She studied his long, tapered fingers as he unconsciously toyed with the silverware beside his plate.

Throughout the dinner he completely ignored her. Starr was alternately angry and humiliated. Never once did he turn in her direction or try to include her in the conversation. As the minutes dragged painfully by, she felt her cheeks grow hotter and hotter. Starr sat silently, willing the unbearable evening to a merciful, quick end.

Finally, Jan glanced at Melissa, who was falling asleep at the table, and suggested that they take the children home. After Jan and Bob had left with the children, Starr started to rise from the booth, but Trevor caught her wrist.

"Stay," he ordered in a low but commanding tone.

Anger welled in her chest at his demand and she tried to pull her arm away, but he held her with a relentless grip.

Millie came by and Trevor ordered another cup of coffee. Starr managed to shake her head when Millie asked if she wanted more tea. Trevor let go of her wrist and a heavy silence settled over the booth.

As Trevor added creamer to his coffee, she could feel his burning gaze on her. Her already upset stomach fluttered in warning. What did he want now? At last she found her voice.

"Trevor, I don't know why you wanted me to stay, but—"

He banged his coffee cup down so hard it rattled the silverware. "Will you just be quiet for a change and listen to me?" he asked harshly.

Biting her lip, Starr fought back the retort that rose automatically to his question.

"All right," she agreed with a long, weary sigh. "What do you want now—another vote for something?"

An angry glint sparked in his green eyes and she felt that she might have pushed him too far this time.

"You're very judgmental for a Christian, Starr Monroe. Maybe your ex-boyfriend made the right decision when he jilted you."

Her face drained of color and she half rose from the booth as her hand made contact with his face. The sound of the blow echoed throughout the restaurant and Millie looked at them in shock. Most of the diners around them had stopped eating and were staring at the two of them with great interest.

His green eyes were afire with unrestrained anger. For an awful moment she thought he was going to strike her in retaliation.

Calmly, he took out his wallet and threw down some bills while Starr remained frozen in the same position. Standing up, he grabbed her arm.

"Come on, slugger," he said caustically as he pulled her out of the booth after him. "Let's finish this in private."

As he dragged her from the restaurant, Starr closed her eyes in disgrace. It wouldn't take long for this episode to get around town. A lot of the local gossips would enjoy this just as much as her being jilted.

Once they were outside the restaurant he continued to drag her along until they reached his car. He opened the door and shoved her into the front seat. Starr saw Millie peeking out the café window and sank lower in the seat.

Trevor slid behind the wheel and started the engine after giving her a look of disgust. He drove out of town without either of them speaking. The big white car moved along the twisting road with ease. Big, silent tears slid down her cheeks as she gazed out the window.

At Turkey Knob, Trevor pulled the car onto the lookout and turned off the motor.

"Starr," he said quietly as he turned her to look at him, "I'm sorry for what I said back in the restaurant about Kevin." He pulled a handkerchief out of his pocket and wiped away her tears. She closed her eyes against his gentle touch but found it was harder to close her heart against the unwanted response it brought.

"That was a low, mean thing for me to say," he admitted, "but I wanted to strike back at you. A few weeks ago I thought that we had found something rare and wonderful, but evidently I was wrong. I've spent the last few weeks wondering why you thought so little of me as to accuse me of trying to bribe you with my affections."

Hope rose suddenly in her heart. "Are you telling me that you didn't use me to get my vote?"

Trevor sighed. "It really doesn't matter now, Starr. The damage is done. You condemned me without hearing my side of the story. I don't think I could ever forget that."

Her heart sank at the hardness in his voice. He hated her. How had she been so wrong about him?

"I wanted you to stay at the restaurant so we could talk about Jan and Bob."

"What about them?"

"This is a wonderful time for them, and our dislike for each other shouldn't cloud the happiest day of their lives. When I saw the tension I was creating by not talking to you at the diner, I realized we would have to make an agreement with each other. I think we should bury the hatchet for one day at least and pretend we can tolerate each other until the wedding is over."

Starr looked straight ahead into the dark night. "Do you think that's possible?" she asked in a small, sad voice.

"Yes. I think we're both adult enough not to want to ruin a special day for two wonderful people. I know it'll be difficult for you to be friendly with someone of my low morals, but I think we owe it to those two lovely people. Bob means a lot to me and I'll do whatever's necessary to make the day a happy one for him."

Even pretending to like me, she thought in silent torment.

"Truce for tomorrow?" he asked, taking her hand.

"Truce," Starr agreed and looked quickly out the window so he wouldn't see her tears.

They didn't speak on the drive back to town, and when he let her out in front of the diner, Trevor made no effort to hold the door.

"Good-night," he said coldly as she got out of the car.

Slamming the door, she hurried away, her tears almost blinding her as she ran toward the safety of her own car.

TWELVE
Old Ties

As Jan came slowly down the aisle, Starr blinked back the tears that threatened to erupt at any second. On the altar a glorious profusion of fall flowers brightened the interior of the old church with a dazzling burst of color. Jan's sister Charlotte hadn't been able to come from Huntington, but it appeared to Starr that everyone in Springfield had shown up for the event.

Reverend Hartford awaited the glowing bride at the altar. He had married her to Frank, Sr., christened her children, and officiated at Frank's funeral. With a beaming smile he stood ready to give his blessing on her new union before God and her friends.

As her heart overflowed with happiness for Jan, Starr glanced at Trevor and was rewarded with a smile. Even if it was only for today, she was glad to be on the receiving end of his dazzling smile. On this wonderful occasion she wanted no shadows cast by anyone.

With nervous fingers Starr smoothed the emerald green dress. The afternoon sun had warmed the church and the long-sleeved velvet dress was fast becoming too warm. Her dark hair was pulled behind her ears and caught with a green velvet bow at the back of her head. A soft black tendril curled gracefully in front of each ear. She stole another glance at Trevor. The black suit he wore gave only the slightest hint of his hard-muscled body. His blond hair curled riotously over the sleek, dark fabric, and she found herself wanting desperately to touch those unruly strands. A sad little sob caught in her throat and Reverend Hartford cast an anxious look at her.

Starr gave the reverend a weak smile and shut her eyes, trying to blot out Trevor's image. As she listened to Bob and Jan exchanging their vows, she couldn't help thinking about what might have been between Trevor and herself. What might have been, her mind tormented.

As Trevor stepped forward to hand Bob the ring, Starr wondered what thoughts were going through his mind. Were those tears in his eyes?

"I now pronounce you man and wife," Reverend Hartford concluded with a satisfied smile. As Bob tenderly kissed his new bride, Starr was unable to hold back the tears any longer. Jan and Bob walked down the aisle toward the outside door with Frank and Melissa following closely behind.

Through the haze of tears, she felt Trevor's hand on her arm.

"I think we're next, Starr," he whispered as he urged her forward.

They stood outside the church blinking in the brilliant sunlit fall day. A horde of well-wishers crowded around the newlywed couple, congratulating the groom and kissing the bride. Acutely aware of Trevor's presence, Starr allowed herself to be borne along in the rush of the crowd into the reception hall.

Inside the packed hall, Trevor continued to hold onto her arm. "You're crying again," he commented as he studied her wet eyes.

"I'm happy," Starr sniffled as she wiped her eyes with an already damp tissue. Someone bumped into her and Trevor caught her quickly.

"You're prettier than the bride," a voice said behind her.

"Kevin!" she gasped as she spun around, nearly knocking the cup of punch from his hand.

Trevor released her arm, nodded curtly to Kevin, and excused himself to extend his congratulations to Bob and Jan. A coil of unhappiness wound in Starr's chest as she watched him go. He seemed eager to be rid of her company.

Reluctantly, she turned her attention to Kevin. "What are you doing here?"

He sipped his punch and smiled at her question. "I didn't crash, honest. Jan invited me."

Starr glanced nervously around the crowded room. She saw surprised expressions on several faces as she and Kevin were observed talking together. The room seemed to grow warmer by the minute, and Starr began edging toward the exit door leading to the garden. Perspiring profusely in the velvet dress, she asked Kevin to excuse her and hurried out the door. On her way out she caught a glimpse of Jan smiling up at Bob with stars in her eyes. Starr was sure she wouldn't be missed for a few moments.

A gentle breeze touched her warm cheeks and she breathed a long sigh of relief. The sweet smell of newly cut grass filled the garden with a heady, earthy aroma, and she inhaled deeply. The tranquillity of the garden had an immediate calming effect on her, and she leaned against a large oak and sipped her punch.

"You do look breathtaking in that dress, Starr."

An audible sigh of frustration slipped from her lips. The sanctuary was violated. Crushing the Styrofoam cup in her hand, she rolled it into tiny pieces.

"Thank you. But it is a bit too warm for this time of year," she told Kevin in a cool, impersonal voice. Reawakening old memories wasn't something she was in the mood for today, of all days.

He moved closer to her under the shade of the big tree.

"It sure is warm," he agreed as he reached out to touch the green bow in her dark hair. "Starr," he whispered in a husky voice as he traced the path of the soft curl in front of her ear, "I want you to know how sorry I am about what happened between us. I'll never quit hating myself for what I did to you."

His agonized eyes beseeched her.

"I believe we've already gone over this, Kevin," she informed him with a resigned sigh.

"I know, but I want you to understand how I feel."

She shut her eyes, wishing he would go away and leave her alone to enjoy the tranquillity of the surroundings.

He gazed thoughtfully past her at something in the distance beyond the church garden. "I know you think I came back to Springfield to awaken old hurts. At first I thought we could pick up where we left off five years ago. But then I realized the Starr I knew had disappeared. I guess we both have changed."

Remaining silent, Starr gazed at the brilliant array of asters that now dominated the church garden. The deep red and purple rays that burst forth from the yellow centers of the fall flowers reminded her of blood and suffering—much like this unexpected and unwanted opening of old wounds.

"There's never been a day in the past five years that I haven't thought about you." He wiped away a tear as it slid quietly down her cheek. "Starr, I hope someday you'll find it in your heart to truly forgive me. I came here today to see you one last time and beg your forgiveness."

She turned wet, questioning eyes to his pain-filled gaze.

"What do you mean?"

"I'm leaving for San Francisco tomorrow. Dad's upset that I don't want to follow in his footsteps in the furniture business, but I have to do this. Maybe if I'm far enough away from family and friends, I can do some growing up." He sighed unhappily. "I've already made one bad marriage. Thank God, there were no children." Gently, he took her face in his hands. "We did mean something to each other once. I guess I wanted to find out if we still did. But I found out that you can't go home again. I'm begging you to find it in your heart to forgive me before I go, Starr. I don't want to spend the rest of my life feeling guilty for what I did."

"You really mean it, don't you?" Starr said in wonder. The truth was reflected in his sad eyes. A euphoric release flooded through her body, lifting her to a glorious high.

"Oh, Kevin, I do forgive you." She took his hand in hers. "In some ways I was as much to blame for what happened to us as you. We just weren't right for each other. We didn't know it—but God did."

"Thanks, Starr. I can go in peace now and start my new life." He bent and kissed her one last time, squeezing her hand in farewell. "Give my best to Jan," he called as he hurried down the path toward the church.

Starr stood staring after him. She felt born anew as the old hurts were washed away in the truth of forgiveness. The unconditional release she had given him had also freed her. From that moment on she could live without being chained to that horrible event in her past.

"Thank you, Lord, for helping me learn what true forgiveness really means," she whispered as she leaned against the rough bark and closed her eyes in happiness.

As peace flooded through her soul, she praised God with all her heart. Although she had told Kevin earlier that he was forgiven, she knew now that it had been lip service only. Deep in her soul she had still been bitter. And hurt. Now the burden raised from her soul, evaporating into the pungent autumn air, freeing her once and for all. A deep sigh of contentment escaped from her.

"Starr?"

Mayor Russell stood at the back door of the reception hall. "Are you out here? They want you inside for the wedding pictures."

"I'm coming," she called as she hurried inside with a much lighter heart.

She smiled and shook hands as she threaded her way toward the wedding group. Her former aloofness had disappeared with the calming of her troubled heart.

Tony Benito, the photographer, was waiting impatiently for her to arrive. At his instructions she took her place beside Trevor.

"Starr, move a little closer to Mr. Hall, please," he ordered.

Trevor's fingers bit into her arm and she looked up in surprise.

The cold look in his eyes shocked her.

"Starr, smile," Tony pleaded. "You look like you're at a funeral instead of a wedding."

As the flashbulb exploded in her eyes, Trevor whispered in her ear, "Did you have a nice time in the garden?"

Anger spread down her arms like liquid fire. "You were spying on me again," she hissed at him.

"Starr, for crying out loud, smile," an exasperated Tony demanded.

She gave him a dazzling smile, but her eyes were blazing.

"Great, Starr. That's it. Thanks, folks."

Immediately the smile disappeared from her face and she turned to glare at Trevor. His hand held her arm like a steel band. Jan had turned to look at the two of them with a questioning expression.

"Be nice," Trevor threatened under his breath. "Smile at me."

Angry beyond belief, Starr did as he ordered, as Trevor pushed her ahead of him toward the garden exit.

"Let me go, you bully," she raged as soon as the door had slammed behind them.

"Gladly," he said as he thrust her away.

With hands on her hips, she turned to face him. "You have your nerve, Trevor Hall. What were you doing, listening and watching all the time I was talking to Kevin? The way you spy on people, you ought to be in the CIA instead of the construction business."

"Talking?" Trevor accused with a lift of a blond eyebrow. "I don't recall too much talking. It seemed more like you were throwing yourself at him."

"Oh, you—you—" Starr vainly searched for an adequate word as her lip trembled in frustration.

"What's the matter, Starr? Does the truth hurt?" Trevor asked as he advanced toward her.

The anger in his eyes frightened her and she backed slowly away, trying to escape his furious glare. One of her heels caught on the cracked stone of the path and she fell as the heel snapped.

"Starr!" Trevor cried in alarm as he ran to help her.

Before he could reach her, she had scrambled to her feet.

"Don't touch me," she screamed as tears streamed down her flushed face. "Stay away from me, Trevor Hall. I hate you," she wailed as she fled from the garden.

For a moment Trevor stood staring after her with a stunned expression. He remained in the garden for several more minutes, gazing at the brilliant blossoms with a perplexed frown. When he finally rejoined the reception, Starr was on her way out.

THIRTEEN
New Twist

After fleeing from Trevor in the church garden, Starr quickly gave her best wishes to Jan and Bob. She pled a headache, but had a suspicion that Jan knew better. Bob's warm eyes empathized with her and he patted her hand in understanding.

"Give Trevor some time," he advised in a gentle voice. "He's under a lot of pressure right now."

Ignoring his comment about Trevor, Starr kissed Bob on the cheek and said, "Take good care of Jan."

Bob smiled as his eyes strayed to Jan's curly red head. "I found a great little lady, didn't I?"

Starr nodded and ran for the hall as she saw Trevor entering the room. One more encounter with him today would be her undoing.

In the privacy of her bedroom Starr looked in the mirror at the sad-faced girl with the puffy red eyes who gazed back with such a forlorn expression. The dress was beautiful, she thought, as she unzipped and tossed it onto the bed, glad to be rid of the heavy material. P.J. immediately snuggled atop the soft velvet.

"P.J., that's brand new!" P.J. purred in contentment and licked her paws. "Oh, well," Starr muttered to herself. "I'll never wear that thing again anyway." It would always remind her of Trevor. And the shoes were ruined. Not even paid for yet. She tossed a mutilated shoe into the corner of the room and P.J. jumped in alarm.

"Sorry, girl," she apologized as she slipped into jeans and a cool T-shirt.

In bare feet she padded out to the kitchen to make herself a tall glass of iced tea. Slamming the ice cubes into the pitcher, she shook with suppressed anger as she thought of Trevor's accusation about Kevin. She stopped with the glass of tea midway to her lips as a horrible thought suddenly occurred to her. Had she been just as guilty of accusing him of something of which he was innocent? For a fleeting moment the possibility stunned her, but she quickly dismissed it. He was guilty all right. He hadn't even bothered to deny it. Nothing could alter that.

If it weren't for Trevor, she'd still be at the wedding reception with her best friend. As angry as she was with him, she still longed to explain about Kevin. Let him think what he wanted, she finally decided. He would anyway.

A cool breeze had begun to blow across the mountains as Starr sat in the swing drinking her iced tea. The silence of the countryside soothed her into a relaxed state and she sat lazily watching the sun sink lower on the horizon. Even the run-in with Trevor didn't diminish the tremendous spiritual glow she felt because of forgiving Kevin. Why Jan had invited him to the wedding was still a mystery, but Starr was glad that she had.

The act of forgiving had cleansed her heart and freed her from years of needless torment. The shame she had carried for the past few years had disappeared.

"God bless you, Kevin," she whispered to the soft breeze, "wherever you may be." Had he never come back into her life she would have carried that awful burden for the rest of her days.

Twilight was just beginning to touch the quiet countryside when Starr reluctantly roused herself from the swing to start the evening chores. As she headed for the barn, she realized that Jan and Bob had probably already left on their honeymoon. Jan had been so thrilled because Trevor had given Bob a week off, even though he was pushing to finish as much of the outside work as possible before cold weather. They were dropping Frank and Melissa off at Jan's sister's in Huntington. The rest of their plans were secret. Starr smiled as she gathered eggs. They were so in love. Ignoring the lump in her throat, she headed for the house to feed Clem and P.J.

She awakened the next morning before the alarm sounded.

"Well," she announced to P.J., who was studying her with quizzical eyes from her perch on the dresser, "there's a lot to be said for following the advice Jesus gave about forgiving our fellowman. I feel like a new person." Much to her amazement she had slept straight through the night and felt wonderfully refreshed.

As she stood waiting for the water in the teakettle to boil, she shut the kitchen window, just barely glancing at the riotous show of oranges and golds that covered the rolling hillside.

At the store, business was brisker than usual and Starr kept busy waiting on customers and taking inventory. By Wednesday morning she was really missing Jan.

"Mornin', Starr," Sam Thomas greeted her as he handed her the mail.

"Good morning, Sam. How's Sue doing?"

"A lot better. Which reminds me, I want to buy some more of those vitamins. She's about out."

Starr placed the small stack of mail to one side and went to the back of the store to get a bottle of B-complex vitamins.

After he paid for his purchase, Sam rested his weary feet and chatted for a while. "Bet you're gonna miss your friend, Jan," he observed, "now that she's got a husband to take care of."

"Going to?" Starr laughed. "I already do!"

"Well," he said, hoisting the heavy mail sack, "best get going before everyone starts complaining about their mail being late."

Starr waved good-bye to him and picked up the mail. The electric bill was always unpleasant news due to the age and inefficiency of the old freezers. She sorted through the remainder of the mail, idly glancing at the numerous bills. A plain white envelope without a return address caught her attention and she opened it. After reading a few lines, she dropped it with a shocked cry of disbelief. Her lease had been canceled! She glanced around the small store in shock. A raise in rent she had expected, but not this! She picked up the letter and read it again. Perhaps she had misunderstood it. No, there was no mistake. She stumbled around the counter and sat down heavily in the bucket chair. She had less than two months to find a new place for her store. This just couldn't be happening!

After the initial shock wore off, Starr went to the back room and dialed Jan's office. Mr. Bowman finally answered.

"I understand your agitation, Starr, but you've known for some time now that the building was up for sale. Mr. Beattie has been trying to get rid of it before he had to spend too much on repairs. Since he doesn't get down here from Huntington that often, it's understandable that he'd like to unload it."

"Well, sure, but why won't the new owner let me renew my lease?" she demanded.

"I believe he wants to convert the building into a restaurant or something. He likes the location."

"A restaurant!" Starr echoed incredulously. "Of all the stupid, idiotic ideas. The café's just a block away!"

"I know, Starr, but it's his prerogative as owner," Mr. Bowman said smoothly, trying to placate her rising temper.

"Well, just who is the new owner? I'm going to tell him what I think of his crazy idea." Her knuckles had turned white from gripping the phone.

"I'm sorry, Starr. I'm not at liberty to say at this point in the transaction."

Taking a deep breath, Starr struggled valiantly to control the rising fury. "Thanks for nothing, Mr. Bowman," she said with an icy venom in her voice as she slammed down the receiver.

"That was plain stupid, Starr," she chastised herself as she headed for the cash register. "Just one more vote you won't get when election time rolls around next year." She was unpopular enough with a wide segment of the voting populace because of her environmental opinions. With 30 percent of the 65,000 coal miners unemployed, most people didn't want to hear about saving the land—they wanted to work. Starr still had hopes that someday both needs could be satisfied.

The afternoon passed in a confused haze as she searched her mind continually for a way out of her current dilemma. Maybe when Jan returned from her honeymoon on Sunday Starr could get the name of the new owner from her. Surely whoever had bought the building wasn't above reason. She would make him see how bad a mistake it was to put a restaurant in this old building. Glancing around the ancient interior, she shuddered. It was impossible to imagine anyone foolish enough to think he could turn this place into an eatery.

Starr refused to give in to the panic that threatened to consume her. If she couldn't talk the new owner into letting her stay, what would she do? She had used her parents' insurance money to open the store three years ago, and although she hadn't grown rich, she was making a living. Well, almost, she amended truthfully. There were still some months when she had to dip into her dwindling savings account, but she tried to remain optimistic in her overall view.

"Lord, help my unbelief," she prayed as the clock finally moved around to five.

When she walked into the council meeting at a quarter till seven, she saw Burton's eyes rise in definite appreciation. She had worn one of her new purchases, a stunning red dress that hugged her tall figure with graceful swirls. The luxurious material swooshed against her legs with a pleasant sensation as she went to the water cooler to fill her glass. She glanced back at Mayor Russell, who was lighting his cigar, and then opened the window. Sal Goldman, who owned the drugstore on Main Street, joined her at the fountain.

"You look terrific in that dress, Starr. Of course, you always do," he added quickly, holding the spigot so she could fill the glass.

"Thanks, Sal." She smiled at the white-haired man with affection. There had been a time when they hadn't gotten along. Right after she opened the health food store, Sal had been terrified that she would take a lot of his business. But they had learned to coexist, and in the last year or so had become good friends.

Starr gave a quick perusal of the other council members. Billy Joe McDaniels was gazing into space with a contemplative look on his round face. Probably dreaming of all the new customers the development would bring into his market. No one was looking at her with a smirk. She had thought for sure that the episode with Trevor at the diner would have made the rounds by now.

John Evers smiled as she sat down beside him. "Jan made a beautiful bride, didn't she?"

Starr nodded as the mayor called the meeting to order. Somewhere in the middle of the discussion about the possibility of hiring an extra deputy for the sheriff's department, Starr became aware that Burton was eyeing her constantly.

Honestly, she thought to herself as she kept her eyes deliberately focused on the mayor, sometimes Burt is so transparent.

As soon as the meeting was over, Starr hurried out into the corridor to escape the smoke-filled room. She stood against the wall trying to clear her lungs of the rank odor.

"Think we should impeach the mayor for his cigar smoking?"

"I don't know, Burt. Sometimes it seems like an awfully good idea. Nothing like getting second-hand lung cancer."

Leaning against the wall, Burton gave her a thorough appraisal. "You should wear red more often. It does wonders for you. That navy blue dress you wear all the time doesn't do you any justice."

Starr blushed. She hadn't thought anyone noticed that she wore the same dress most of the time.

"Thanks, Burt. Jan talked me into buying some new clothes when we went shopping for wedding dresses."

"Ah, yes. Jan, the blushing bride."

An unpleasant shiver coursed through her body. There was always an undercurrent in Burton's voice that she disliked.

Starr turned to leave.

"I hear you had a little row with your boyfriend the other night at the diner."

She froze in her tracks for a moment before taking a deep breath and turning to face him again. So the silence was too good to be true. She should have known she could count on Burton to know everything that happened in the community.

"If you're referring to Trevor Hall, Burton, he's not my boyfriend. To be honest, we can't stand each other."

"I guess he's not as smart as I thought, then," Burton conceded.

"What do you mean?"

"I just found out from Mayor Russell that Hall's not going to clear much profit on this project."

Starr stared at Burton with a dumbfounded expression. "What?" she asked in a tiny whisper.

"Why don't we have some coffee?" Burton said, taking her arm. "I'll tell you what I found out."

At the diner, Millie gave Starr a conspiratorial wink and brought her tea without waiting for the order. Starr sipped the tea slowly, waiting for Burton to elaborate.

"I heard Kevin O'Riley left town for good," he commented in an offhand manner.

Starr curbed her tongue. Burton loved gossip. If she angered him, she'd never find out what he knew about Trevor.

"Yes," she said with a sweet smile. "I spoke with him at Jan's wedding. He has a good job offer in California."

Burton smiled at her over his coffee cup, showing his perfect, white teeth. An image of a Cheshire cat leaped into Starr's mind as she watched him.

"I heard he came back to town because he's still in love with you."

"You heard wrong," Starr corrected, never losing the saccharine smile pasted on her face. "He came back to wrap up some loose ends."

"Including you?"

"In a way. But I'd like to know more about what you found out from the mayor about the project," she prodded.

Burton smiled and signaled Millie for more coffee. Starr declined more tea as she anxiously waited for Millie to move out of hearing range.

The smug smile spread. "I thought you weren't interested in Trevor Hall."

Starr fought back the urge to scream at him. "I'm not, but since I voted for the development against my better judgment, I'm interested in knowing what you found out."

"Mr. Hall is over budget. The mayor said that he has been in California for the last few weeks trying to raise enough money to finish the project. Sold off part of one of his businesses there, I guess, to keep this deal going. From what I gathered, he went into this thing knowing he couldn't make much money from it."

A horrible knot was beginning to twist in Starr's stomach as she thought of how she had called him money hungry.

"I sure had some wrong ideas about him," Burton continued. "I thought he was out to bribe the whole council to support his project so he could make a fortune. Then I find out the project is a low-cost housing development for older people. Sort of an experimental concept that he designed himself. He couldn't purchase the land cheap enough in California or get enough state or federal aid to supplement it. With our natural energy resources here in West Virginia and the subsidy financing from the state government, he was able to go ahead. Yesterday I went out to look at what's been done so far and it's going to be fabulous! You ought to see it, Starr. Gorgeous little townhouses with individual gardens, patios—the whole works."

Starr was feeling sicker by the minute. The

accusations she had made on their first date rose to haunt her with every word Burton said. How wrong she had been about Trevor.

"I really admire the guy for taking a chance on an experimental idea like that, not knowing whether or not he could break even. If he succeeds, it'll bring a lot of new economic life into this community."

"You mean other than for the people working on the project?"

"Yes. It's designed primarily for federal retirees, retired military personnel, or any local people of retirement age who have worked in some government area. We'll have new people coming into Springfield and they'll be spending money at our local stores and putting money into our banks, buying cars, clothing, groceries. You name it. We're all going to reap the benefits of this baby."

"So when he asked for council votes it really wasn't for his own gain?" Starr asked in a strained voice.

"I guess not," Burton concurred. "He just didn't tell us all the details of the concept. Maybe he was afraid we wouldn't want an influx of new people in town. I don't know."

Suddenly Starr had to escape from Burton and go examine her own thoughts in privacy. "Thanks for the tea, Burt," she murmured as she gathered her purse and notes from the council meeting. She rushed past Millie, who gave her a surprised look. Poor Millie, Starr thought. She probably thinks I fight with every man in town.

Instead of driving toward home, she headed in the direction of Turkey Knob. Pulling onto the lookout, she turned off the headlights and sat in the car for a few minutes, glad that the night concealed her. She got out of the car and stood looking below. From what she could see in the dark, a lot of construction had been completed in the last two weeks. Some night lights were visible, but from the top of the lookout it was impossible to tell what the buildings actually looked like.

As she gazed at the stars high above, Starr shivered. They glistened like diamonds on a black velvet cloth. Reverting to her childhood pastime, she wished on the brightest one and held her breath.

"Star light, star bright," a soft voice said from behind her.

"Oh," she gasped as she turned in fright, nearly stumbling over the edge.

"Hey, watch it. That's a long drop." Trevor grabbed her by the shoulders as she blinked up at him with disbelief. "Or do you always fall for me?" he asked, referring to her ungraceful plop in the church garden.

"What are you doing here?" she managed to stammer inanely, intensely aware of his strong grip on her arms.

He released her. "I might ask you that same question. It seems as if I always find you trespassing on my property. I saw your lights when you pulled in and came up to check."

She remained silent, caught in the magic of the starlit night with the wind whistling through the trees. In the distance an owl hooted, and she breathed a sigh of contentment.

Trevor leaned against the hood of her car and stared at the lights in the valley below.

"I talked to Burton Hollis after the council meeting tonight," she said, breaking the silence of the peaceful night.

"Oh?"

"He told me about the nature of your project. That it was for retirees and that you weren't going to make any profit on it."

He remained silent.

He certainly wasn't making it any easier for her to tell him what a fool she'd been. "I guess I was wrong about everything, Trevor. I'm sorry."

Suddenly his arms were around her and she was being crushed in his powerful embrace. His lips sought hers in a warm, searching probe of tenderness, and her arms slid around his neck to grasp the silky thick hair in her fingers. She could hear the rapid thudding of his heart and she pressed closer to him, drunk with the joy of his nearness.

Abruptly, he thrust her away. "I was wrong about you too, Starr," he said with a coldness that penetrated her bone marrow.

She stared at the vague outline of his face in the dark. "What do you mean?"

"You're not the sweet little country girl I thought you were. You sure had me fooled."

"I had you fooled," she repeated, unable to comprehend his meaning.

Trevor gave a nasty laugh. "It hasn't been three days since I saw you kissing your old beau, and yet you weren't exactly fighting me off just now."

Despite the coolness of the night, her cheeks burned with humiliation. "You're wrong, Trevor," she insisted in a quiet voice. "It wasn't what you thought with Kevin."

"No, you're wrong, Starr. You assumed I was nothing short of a crook, without a shred of proof. You were afraid to trust me and judged me without ever giving me a chance to defend myself."

Without another word he walked away from her into the dark night.

"You're wrong, Trevor," she repeated as she listened to his retreating footsteps. "Now we're both guilty of the same offense."

After Trevor left, Starr stood on the hill for a long time watching the lights flickering across the valley. The cool autumn wind dried her tears and she headed for home.

FOURTEEN
Confessions

For the rest of the week Starr moved through her daily activities like a robot. Answering only when spoken to, she buried herself in work at the store and at home. Even Clem and P.J. failed to lift her spirits, and, sensing her mood, stayed out of her way.

With a heavy heart she prepared for church on Sunday. She wore the French blue suit that Jan had talked her into buying on their shopping spree. As she studied her reflection in the mirror, she decided it was indeed a lovely outfit, but it did nothing to perk up her spirits.

Why, she asked herself as she slammed the dresser drawer shut, does he have this hold on me? She had just cleared her mind of Kevin, and now Trevor's words nagged at her constantly.

Awake or asleep, she thought of him. If she tried to explain that she had been only kissing Kevin good-bye, he wouldn't believe her. Because she hadn't trusted him, she was experiencing the same pangs he'd suffered. And the horrible truth about the whole situation haunted her. He was right—she had judged him without a shred of evidence.

The day was crisp and clear, hinting of much cooler weather to come, she thought, as she hurried into church. The pews in the rear were filled, so Starr hurried down the aisle seeking a vacant seat just as the choir finished singing. As Reverend Hartford stepped to the pulpit and smiled down at her, she slid into the front row.

"Today's sermon," he began, "is entitled 'Does God Want Us to Make a Profit?'" He smiled at his overflowing congregation.

"Many of us have been taught that it's a sin to be rich. That only the poor gain admittance to the kingdom of heaven. But, dear friends, that's wrong. Didn't Jesus himself teach that God wants us to handle well what he gives us?"

An alarm sounded in Starr's brain and she listened intently.

Reverend Hartford started in on the Bible story:

"Jesus said that the kingdom of heaven can be illustrated by the story of a man going into another country, who called together his servants and loaned them money to invest for him while he was gone.

"He gave five thousand dollars to one, two thousand to another, and one thousand to the last—dividing it in proportion to their abilities—and then left on his trip.

"The man who received the five thousand dollars began immediately to buy and sell with it and soon earned another five thousand. The man with two thousand dollars went right to work, too, and earned another two thousand. But the man who received the thousand dollars dug a hole in the ground and hid the money for safekeeping.

"After a long time their master returned from his trip and called them to him to account for his money.

"The man to whom he had entrusted the five thousand dollars brought him ten thousand.

"His master praised him for his good work. 'You have been faithful in handling this small amount,' he told him, 'so now I will give you more responsibilities. Begin the joyous tasks I have assigned to you.'

"Next came the man who had received the two thousand, with the report, 'Sir, you gave me two thousand dollars to use, and I have doubled it.'

"'Good work,' his master said. 'You are a good and faithful servant. You have been faithful over this small amount, so now I will give you much more.'

"Then the man with the thousand dollars came and said, 'Sir, I knew you were a hard man, and I was afraid you would rob me of what I earned, so I hid your money in the earth, and here it is!'

"But his master replied, 'Wicked man! Lazy slave! Since you knew I would demand your profit, you should have at least put my money into the bank so I could have some interest! Take the money from this man and give it to the man with the ten thousand dollars.

"'For the man who uses well what he is given shall be given more, and he shall have abundance. But from the man who is unfaithful, even what little responsibility he has shall be taken from him.'"

Starr felt as though she could barely breathe. How wrong she had been. This was what Trevor had meant when he told her it was hard to be a Christian and a good businessman.

Reverend Hartford continued with his sermon. "I tell you, good people, only when you make God the chairman of your board will you find peace of mind. God wants, yes, God **demands** that you make a profit from the money he has entrusted you with—but," he paused for effect and looked at his attentive congregation, "the ultimate goal in making money is to use it to serve others. Take the profits from your businesses and give it back to those who have not learned to use their money as well. Give it to the poor, the needy, the homeless. Give it back to your Source and it will come back multiplied again to you. Do not make money your god, for it will corrupt you if you lose sight of its purpose. Use it to be of service, and it will always return to you in abundance."

Starr's mind was whirling as she stood to sing the closing hymn.

At the door, as she shook hands with Reverend Hartford, she said, "I can't tell you how much I appreciated your sermon, Reverend, or how much I learned from it."

He smiled and clasped her hands in his. "I saw a lot of happy expressions on our business folks' faces," he beamed. "I'm glad you enjoyed it so much, my dear. Always nice to see you—especially in the front row where you have to be good."

Starr laughed at the reverend's humor as she hurried down the steps toward her car.

The words of his sermon returned to her often that afternoon as she sat in front of the fireplace watching the flames flicker. The morning's sun had disappeared without warning and a cold autumn rain was falling slowly, but with a determined patter, on the roof. She snuggled closer to the fire as she watched Clem and P.J. sleeping in front of the fireplace.

She had certainly been in error about Trevor. He was giving his money back to help people as God intended. Remorse filled her as she thought of how she had judged him so harshly. She had always tried to help others; but she had often been guilty of being too critical, and her caustic tongue had been tempered slowly and painfully through the years.

She opened the Bible to the passages that Reverend Hartford had used as the text for his sermon and reread them in the quietness of the warm living room. When she had finished, she laid the Bible aside and stared into the fireplace. Trevor was a far better Christian than she. Without publicly proclaiming his deeds, he was doing what God had commanded.

She fell asleep in front of the fireplace thinking of Trevor.

Rain was still falling in heavy gray sheets Monday morning. Starr shivered under her umbrella as she unlocked the door to the store. As soon as she entered the building, a strange odor assailed her sensitive nose.

"Oh, no," she cried as she headed for the large freezer at the rear of the store. With trepidation she opened the door and found all the frozen foods warm and soggy. The old freezer had finally died.

Jan found her sobbing and filling the large trash container when she arrived a little after ten.

Rising up from her task, Starr took one look at Jan's radiant face and immediately broke into a loud wail.

"Starr, honey, what's wrong?" Jan's big brown eyes were filled with concern.

Starr sobbed and hiccuped simultaneously. "All this stuff is ruined. I'm ruined. I don't have any place to go!"

"Sit down," Jan ordered as she led Starr to the back room and put on the teakettle. "Now what are you talking about? I've been gone for a week and you're talking disaster."

Starr wiped her eyes and blew her nose with the tissue Jan handed her. Her sobbing abated somewhat as Jan gave her a cup of tea.

"H-how was your honeymoon?" Starr stammered as she sipped the hot tea.

"Wonderful," Jan replied with an ecstatic smile. "Although I have to admit I did miss my little monsters. But enough about me. What are you talking about—no place to go?"

"I've lost my lease."

Jan's brown eyes grew wide with shock. "You're kidding?"

"I was waiting for you to get back. I called Mr. Bowman and he said he couldn't tell me the name of the new owner. That moron wants to have a restaurant here and he wants me out in less than two months. I can't find a place to move to in that short a time!"

Starr's blue eyes were a study in misery and dejection.

Jan shook her head in sympathy. "I'll see what I can find out at the office, Starr. But if Mr. Bowman doesn't want the information released yet, I don't know what I can do."

Starr nodded mutely and ran her fingers through her long black hair, smoothing the heavy curls away from her perspiring brow "Let me know as soon as you can. I'd like to know how long I have before filing bankruptcy."

"Oh, Starr, it's not that bad."

"It will be."

After Jan left for her office, Starr returned to the task of discarding her ruined inventory. It was like watching the dollars go into the trash. With each package she fought back the tears.

She had just finished dragging the trash cans out behind the store when the phone rang in the back room.

"Feeling better?" Jan asked.

"No," Starr admitted truthfully.

"Bob and I want you to come to dinner tonight. We'd like for you to be the first guest we entertain as a married couple."

Starr was about to refuse, but the happiness in Jan's voice swayed her. "Are you sure you want me? I'll be miserable company."

Jan laughed. "That's what friends are for, dummy. Maybe we can lift your spirits or at least find some way out of this mess for you."

Suddenly suspicious, Starr asked, "You're not inviting anyone else, are you?"

"Starr Monroe, you don't trust me," Jan accused. "No, I didn't invite Trevor, if that's what you're thinking."

"OK, I'll come then," she agreed.

"You'll feel better if you do. You shouldn't be alone when you're feeling so low."

"I'll come, but I seriously doubt that I'll feel better."

"That doesn't sound like the Starr I know."

"The Starr you knew wasn't going bankrupt."

"You're impossible. By the way, I checked on that lease. I'm sorry, Starr, but I'm not allowed to give you any information. Mr. Bowman's orders."

"That's all right. I just realized I can check at the courthouse when the deed is recorded."

"Well, fine. I'm glad that's settled."

"It seems strange that Mr. Bowman—" Starr began.

"See you tonight, Starr. Have to go. I have a customer."

To compound her financial woes, the rain continued all day in a heavy downpour. By four thirty only two customers had been in so Starr decided to close early.

The rain beat with a vicious staccato on the small car as Starr crept along the rain-slicked road toward home. She turned the windshield wipers on high, but still had trouble picking out the road in front of her. Perhaps she should call Jan and cancel for tonight. The idea of driving back into town in the heavy deluge of rain wasn't appealing at the moment.

Clem was waiting on the front porch when she pulled into the driveway.

"Oh, Clem, you're a mess!" Just as Starr reached the porch, Clem decided to shake the excess water and mud from her long fur. Looking down at her mud-splattered clothes, Starr started to scold the big dog. But she looked so miserable as her sad brown eyes peered up at Starr that she broke into laughter.

"Oh, darling," she whispered, kissing the damp nose, "you've had a bad day too, haven't you?"

P.J. watched them from the kitchen window with a disdainful expression. Getting wet was definitely not P.J.'s idea of fun.

An hour later a towel-dried Clem lay dozing in front of a roaring fire. As Starr scratched her ears, the big dog emitted an occasional burp of contentment. How nice it would be to solve her own problems so easily, Starr thought as she gazed into the fire with a morose expression.

The rain had stopped shortly after she arrived home.

"Well," she said to Clem, "I guess I'd better change clothes and get ready to visit the newlyweds. Think you can hold down the fort, girl?"

Clem's tail thumped in answer.

Dressed in tan corduroy slacks and a long-sleeved red sweater, Starr headed for Jan's with anything but a light heart.

Bob greeted her at the door with a big hug as Frank and Melissa bubbled over with excitement to tell her about their week with Aunt Charlotte in Huntington.

"Whoa!" Starr exclaimed as she gave her jacket to Bob. "One at a time, please."

Clad in jeans and a deep green sweater, Jan was busy dishing up dinner, but declined Starr's help. "The kids have missed you. Better let them get it out of their systems now or we'll never be able to hear a word at the table."

Starr sat on the couch between Frank and Melissa as they competed for her attention. Her head was spinning from the effort of listening to both of them at the same time.

"Ready, Starr?" Bob asked, poking his head through the doorway.

Both of the children wanted to sit by Starr at dinner so they could continue their non-stop account of their exciting week.

Jan apologized for the chicken.

"Forget it," Starr said as she reached for a biscuit. "I've given up on converting for a while."

"Jan said something about your losing your lease," Bob said as he passed the green beans.

"Probably my shirt along with it."

"Is it that bad, Starr?" His soft brown eyes were filled with concern.

His tenderness unleashed her emotions. Frank and Melissa looked on in amazement as Starr broke into tears.

"Don't cry, Aunt Starr," Frank pleaded as he patted her face with his little hand.

Starr only cried harder as Jan sent the children into the living room to watch television.

"I'm sorry," Starr apologized after she had managed to regain some of her composure.

Jan and Bob sat across from her with worry etched on their serious faces.

"It seems to be my year for making a fool of myself," Starr remarked with a weak attempt at a smile. "I found out from Burton Hollis at the council meeting that Trevor's project is not at all what I thought. I not only was wrong in accusing him of using me to insure my vote, but I was in error about his motives regarding the community."

Bob sighed in relief. "You know then why Trevor returned to California?"

Starr nodded. "Yes. Burton told me he was trying to raise financing to finish the project."

"Now you know the whole truth about the project."

"It doesn't matter, anyway," Starr said as she gazed around the small kitchen with tear-glazed eyes. "He hates me."

"Why don't you go to Trevor and tell him the truth? Admit you were wrong and ask him to forgive you?" Jan asked.

Starr gave a hollow laugh. "I've already tried that. He can't stand the sight of me."

Bob started to say something, then changed his mind as he exchanged a guarded look with Jan.

"And then he saw Kevin kissing me at your wedding. He thinks I'm—" She couldn't finish the statement.

"Oh, Starr, that's my fault," Jan said with a horror-stricken expression. "I invited him only because I wanted you to be finally free of him. He called me and told me he was leaving town. He wanted to see you and was afraid you wouldn't let him after what happened at your house when Trevor came by. I'm so sorry. I never dreamed it would work out like this."

"Don't blame yourself. It worked out fine. I finally have cleansed my mind of Kevin. When Trevor saw Kevin kissing me, it was a good-bye kiss. He's gone to San Francisco for good."

"Oh," Jan breathed in relief.

Starr left shortly after dinner. Bob had to be at the construction site at dawn the following morning and Starr was relieved to have an excuse to leave early.

The next day Jan dropped into the store at lunch.

"Did you have any insurance on your stock, Starr?" she asked as she unwrapped her sandwich.

Starr shook her head. "No, I was cutting corners on the money and decided I couldn't afford any more insurance premiums."

"Ooh," Jan commiserated as she bit into her sandwich. "Too bad."

"Tell me something new," she said drily.

"Can it be fixed?" Jan suggested.

"No, but maybe I could sell it to the Smithsonian." Starr's wry tone didn't escape Jan's notice.

"Well, I'm glad to see your sense of humor's returning."

"Yeah, I'll be a barrel of laughs on my way to the poor house."

"Starr," Jan interrupted suddenly, "I really think you should talk to Trevor."

Starr shook her head and bent down to concentrate on the open book on the counter. "I don't want to talk about him," she insisted firmly, closing the subject.

Jan tossed her wrapper into the wastebasket. "OK, hon. But I think you're making a mistake."

Starr kept her head down.

"See you around," Jan called as she left.

Starr waved with an absent-minded gesture and returned to her work.

Drier weather had returned by midweek, but the cold rain had left its imprint on the land. The golden maples had shed nearly all their leaves, and they stood barren and lonely, silhouetted against the gray sky.

On Thursday morning business was a little more brisk than usual and Starr's hopes rose slightly as she made out the bank deposit.

A daily check at the courthouse had yielded nothing regarding her lease. The mysterious new landlord was keeping a low profile. But sooner or later, she'd find out who he was.

It had better be sooner, she thought as she slipped on her red windbreaker and headed for the bank. Even if she could find a place on such short notice, it would be rough to move when the weather was bad. She would put the situation in God's hands and let him handle it as he saw fit.

"Everything in divine order," she reassured herself as she tried to push aside her anxious thoughts. The sun had begun to set earlier and she shivered as she dropped the deposit in the night slot at the bank.

Business out of the way for the day, she decided to take Burton's advice and drive to the construction site to see what the development looked like. The worst thing that could happen to her was to get thrown off the property by Trevor for trespassing.

As soon as she arrived, she noticed a fire truck and an ambulance. Fear suddenly gripped her, making her knees tremble as she tried to get out of the car.

She rushed past the fireman who stood intently watching a great number of men digging frantically with shovels and some with their hands.

"Miss," the fireman called out to her, "you can't go in that area. There's been a cave-in."

Starr sank to her knees as the fireman caught her.

"Please," he asked, pulling her away. "We're doing everything we can."

Starr stood helplessly by, watching the men

dig. Her eyes searched desperately for a glimpse of Trevor. Finally she spotted Bob and broke away from the fireman.

"Bob," she shouted as he stopped digging for a moment. The only sound that could be heard was the heavy breathing of the men as they dug and the scrape of shovels against the dirt. The ambulance crew waited with their emergency equipment ready.

"Bob," she cried, grabbing his arm, "is it—?"

"Yes, Starr. It's Trevor, and a local man."

Her knees buckled as though she had been struck with a physical blow and the ground came up to meet her as a million stars exploded in her brain.

Seconds later, when she regained consciousness, she heard the elated shouts of several of the men.

"We've found them!"

Too weak to stand, Starr remained on the ground as Trevor and another man were lifted from the mass of loose dirt. Not an eyelash flickered as Starr stared at his still face. Dirt covered his entire body. His eyelids were caked with it and his long blond hair was matted until it was almost impossible to tell the color.

Pain filled every fiber of her being as she watched the ambulance attendants spring into action. Quickly they cleared his nose and mouth of debris and covered his face with an oxygen mask.

As the two men were loaded into the ambulance, Starr found the strength to stand at last.

"Please," she begged the attendant, "may I ride to the hospital with him?"

"You his wife?" he asked as she held Trevor's hand.

"No," she whispered, "just his friend."

"OK, honey, climb in. We're leaving."

On the long ride to the hospital Starr prayed with all her heart as she sat holding Trevor's lifeless hand.

"Oh, Trevor, I love you," she told him again and again as tears dripped from her eyes onto his chest. "Dear God, don't let him die. Please, God, he'll never know that I love him."

She sat shaking in the emergency room as her stomach jerked with spasms of anxiety. Bob joined her and sat holding her hand tightly in his. Dirt still clung to his clothing and his brown beard.

"What happened?" Starr finally managed to ask.

"Trevor and Dale Loomis were checking an excavated area because of all the rain, when all of a sudden the whole thing just caved in. No warning. In a second they were swallowed by the earth." Bob's usually calm voice broke and Starr held him, trying to erase the horror of what he'd seen.

"I've seen it happen before," he continued. "Usually—" he stopped and Starr shuddered at what he left unsaid. "I sounded the alarm and we all started digging like mad. It was a miracle that we found them that quick. And alive."

"A miracle," Starr repeated. "Bob," she urged, "let's go to the hospital chapel and pray."

Heads bowed and hands clasped, they sat a few minutes later in the tiny chapel and prayed for God to spare Trevor and Dale. For the first time since she'd driven to the construction site earlier that evening, Starr felt a calmness invade her.

"Go home, Bob," she told him as they left the chapel. "You look exhausted. I'll stay here. I promise to call as soon as I hear anything." It took her several minutes to convince him, but at last he reluctantly went home to Jan.

When Starr returned to the emergency waiting room, she discovered that Trevor had been moved to a room on the second floor. She took the elevator upstairs and settled down for a long wait. Much to her surprise, a few minutes later a young man in a white jacket approached her.

"Are you Starr?" he asked.

"Yes." She jumped quickly to her feet.

"Mr. Hall has been asking to see you."

"Is he—?"

"We think he's going to be fine. He's a very lucky young man. They both are. But they're badly bruised and disoriented. I'll warn you Mr. Hall is very much out of it right now but he insists on seeing you."

Her heart was leaping with fear and excitement.

"Don't stay more than a minute," he warned.

As she opened the door to his room, her knees started to shake again. She approached the bed with great apprehension. His usually dark face was pale and so still. The dark lashes lay motionless against his cheeks.

Starr's teeth began to chatter in fright as she reached for his hand.

With great effort Trevor opened his eyes. "Starr," he murmured, "wanted you to know—" His eyes closed and she started to cry softly.

When he didn't say anything more the nurse put her hand firmly on Starr's back. "You'd better go, dear. He needs to rest."

She turned at the door to take one final look at him.

"Good-bye, my love," she whispered and then fled from the room.

She called Bob and Jan from home to report on Trevor's condition. Wrapping herself in a quilt, she stretched out on the sofa for what she knew would be a long, sleepless night.

FIFTEEN
Peace

As soon as she awakened from a fitful slumber Friday morning, Starr called the hospital and was told that both men were greatly improved.

"Glory to God," she whispered and bowed her head in thanks.

Friday and Saturday proved to be the longest days of her life. She found it impossible to think about anything but Trevor. Her youth group was meeting at the reclamation site on Sunday afternoon, and she had decided to visit Trevor after that. She knew now that she loved him with all her heart and soul—which made it all the more frightening to face him, knowing how he felt about her.

After church, Starr rounded up the group, trying to determine who was driving and who needed a ride. When they arrived at the site, they were saddened at the vast amount of damage the heavy rains had inflicted.

Joe stood by Starr's car looking at the area with a downcast expression. "It looks terrible again," he complained.

As Starr viewed the newly eroded ground, she was forced to agree with him. It was horrid looking.

"Well," she said to the depressed faces that were turned to her for guidance, "at least it isn't all gone. We'll just have to raise more money in the spring and try again."

"Oh, Starr," Laura said as her big brown eyes filled with tears, "it's so heartbreaking. Doesn't God know we want to make this land beautiful again?"

"I'm sure he does, Laura. We don't always know why these things happen. We just have to keep on trying."

The group wandered around the area picking up rocks and other debris that the rain had washed down from the mountains. A deep sadness filled Starr as she looked at the mutilated land. The ugly scars were once more visible. Their efforts had been for nothing.

A few minutes later she sent them all home. There was nothing any of them could do right then to rectify the damage. Lost in thought, she leaned against the hood of her car and surveyed the mess with a heavy heart.

"Still think I'd do this to the land?" a soft voice inquired from behind her.

Starr whirled around to see Trevor slowly making his way toward her. Her heart raced wildly as she stared at him, unable to believe that it was really he.

Her eyes flew to his pale face. "You're in the hospital!" she exclaimed. "I mean, you're supposed to be!"

"Not anymore. I threw such a fit they were glad to get rid of me."

"How did you know I was here?"

"Reverend Hartford told me. You'd already left with your group by the time I got to church."

Starr stood rooted to the spot as he walked toward her and lifted her black hair from her face as the wind tugged at it. An incredible look of longing filled his eyes as he continued to stare down at her. The autumn afternoon was turning cool and her cheeks had a soft pink hue.

He gazed into her blue eyes for a long moment.

"You didn't answer my question. Do you think I'd be guilty of doing this to the land?"

"No," she murmured as she dropped her eyes from his penetrating gaze. His nearness made her legs tremble.

"You should have worn a jacket," he scolded as he unzipped his and slid it around her shoulders. His gentle touch completely unnerved her.

"You should keep your jacket," she protested. "You'll suffer a relapse. I don't even think you should be out of the hospital."

"That's what the doctor said," Trevor agreed with a wide grin, "but I told him I had something that had to be done."

Starr broke into laughter. "You're impossible."

"I think I've heard that before."

Swaying slightly, he asked, "Did I tell you anything in the hospital?"

"You do remember me being there?" she whispered in amazement.

"Yes. Did I manage to tell you anything before I conked out?"

"No."

"I was trying to tell you that I plan on staying permanently in West Virginia. I'm moving my construction company here."

Little tremors of shock registered throughout her body. "S-stay?" she stammered.

"I knew when I went back to California that I'd found the right girl. I plan to settle down here with her." His eyes grew dreamy as he looked at the rolling hills in the distance.

Starr felt as though a giant hand was crushing the very life from her. He had met someone in California. Utter despair filled her and she turned away from him so he couldn't see the sudden rush of tears.

"Yep," Trevor continued, "I've never felt as much at home anywhere else as I do here. There's something about this land that gets in your blood."

"I'm happy for you," Starr finally managed to whisper through her tears.

Trevor gave her a puzzled look. "Happy for

me? Is that all you have to say when a guy gives up his home, his business, and moves twenty-five hundred miles to be with you?"

"What?" Her head snapped to attention as her eyes grew round with wonder.

Trevor tilted her head back and gazed into the shocked blue eyes. Kissing her cold cheeks, he whispered, "What about it, Starr? Will you marry me?"

Her lips parted but she couldn't utter a single word as she stared dumbfounded into his twinkling green eyes.

Trevor cradled her in his arms. "Jan told me about Kevin. I'm sorry I jumped to the wrong conclusion, but you have to realize I was eaten up with jealousy. Can you ever forgive me, Starr?"

Nestling in the warmth of his arms, she sighed and rested her head against his shoulder. "If you'll forgive me."

"You're forgiven. And I have to admit I did deliberately provoke you on several occasions."

She jerked away. "You what?" she thundered as her blue eyes snapped. "You **deliberately**—"

As Trevor rolled his eyes heavenward, Starr broke into laughter.

"I guess," Trevor said with a sigh, "I'm never going to have a boring moment with you."

Later that evening as they sat in Starr's living room, he told her about the cave-in.

"As I lay there thinking I was going to die, I kept promising God if he'd just let me have another chance, I'd give all my life to him—not just a part. No more backsliding. No more halfway attempts at being a good Christian. I prayed like I'd never prayed in my entire life. As my life's breath was being crushed from me, I kept pleading with God to let me live. 'Let me live so I can tell Starr how much I love her. Let me live so we can see our children born and raised to serve God.'"

Starr was crying openly, not trying to hold back the deluge of hot tears as she imagined Trevor pinned beneath that mound of earth, gasping for breath and pleading with God.

"And then in the ambulance," Trevor continued, "I thought I was dreaming or dead when I heard you say you loved me. I was sure I wanted to hear it so bad that I was hallucinating. I couldn't figure out how you could be there with me."

Starr tried to staunch the flow of tears but gave up. "You did hear me. You were so still...." Fear gripped her anew as she remembered his deathly stillness in the ambulance.

Trevor squeezed her hand until she thought it would break. "I could hear you but I couldn't answer. My eyes wouldn't open. Everything seemed to be far away. I guess that's why I kept telling the doctor at the hospital that I had to see you. I was afraid I was going to die and you'd never know how much I love you."

They looked at each other in wondrous delight.

"Oh, Trevor," Starr said, wiping away her tears, "if I'd lost you—"

"Shh," he ordered, kissing her tears away. "Don't think about it."

They were interrupted by P.J. nestling between them on the sofa. Trevor raised a dubious eyebrow as the cat kneaded his pants with her claws. Clem lay dozing by the blazing fire, her legs twitching as she dreamed of some exciting adventure.

"We're not taking these two with us on our honeymoon, are we?" he asked as he removed P.J. to the other end of the sofa where she glared at him for having the audacity to disturb her.

"No. I think I can talk Jan into watching them while we're gone. Are you sure you want to leave your work? We can always go later," she assured him. "I wouldn't mind."

"Bob can manage without me for a couple of weeks. Where did you have in mind? Paris? Rome?"

Opening her eyes for a brief, lazy second, Starr gave him an enigmatic smile. "Oh, some place I think you'll like much better."

With a wicked wink Trevor said, "I can see it all now. Reverend Hartford will ask me if I promise to love, honor, and eat my veggies for the rest of my life."

"Funny," Starr told him as she shoved his feet off of the coffee table. "I know when I'm beaten. You're the original immovable object."

"Me! I'm putty in your hands, my dear. Just

think of the lifetime challenge you'll face in reforming me. In the still of the night I'll be sneaking out to the nearest McDonald's."

Starr barely managed to suppress a giggle as Trevor pulled her into his arms.

"I still think," she murmured against his chest, "that you could have told me about your project from the beginning."

"I couldn't. I might have lost the financing if word had leaked out before the deal was concrete."

"But that first night at the restaurant you let me think those horrible things about you." Her cheeks turned pink as she thought about the caustic remarks she'd made.

"I wasn't exactly guiltless, Starr. If you will recall, I said some pretty mean things myself. What was it I called you?"

"You know full well what you called me. 'Unreasonable little hillbilly.'"

"Some things never change, do they?" Trevor teased as he dodged her hand and caught it to his lips.

"You know," he whispered as he kissed her fingers, "I'll never let you get away, Starr. I remember that first day I saw you on your hands and knees picking your posies. I knew you were special even then. How strange that I had to come over two thousand miles to find my little hillbilly."

Starr gazed into his eyes as though she would never tire of probing those teasing green depths. "God planned it that way," she told him. "I feel so bad now when I think of all the time I spent being angry with God over what had happened with Kevin."

Trevor looked at her in surprise. "You never told me you felt that way."

"I didn't really know it until that day in the church garden when Kevin asked me to forgive him and I felt God's love in my heart after releasing my hate and fear."

"We owe Kevin a lot," Trevor said.

"We owe God a lot," Starr corrected as she nestled once again in the arms where she belonged.

SIXTEEN
A New
Landlord

The attractive young couple stood with their arms linked around each other as they gazed at the grandeur of the magnificent falls rushing beneath them. Clad in heavy winter coats, they stood alone in the primitive setting as they marveled at the majestic power of nature.

Starr turned to Trevor, her cheeks glowing as much from happiness as from the sting of the cold wind.

"Did you know that the Indians thought West Virginia was too rugged for anyone to inhabit and they came here only to hunt and fish and use the healing springs?"

Trevor gave an appreciative whistle as he eyed the rough terrain. "I can believe that."

During the past few days they had explored the backwoods and scenic wonders of Starr's home state.

"You're the most God-and-country-and-apple-pie person I've ever encountered," Trevor had grumbled good-naturedly as Starr dragged him to look at the largest sycamore tree in the world near Webster Springs. They had relived John Brown's execution and toured the wax museum at historic Harper's Ferry. On a backwoods road in wondrous silence they had observed a young fawn running with his mother as they stood awestruck before such perfect innocence and beauty.

Trevor's admiration for the land was increasing daily, as was his love for the dark-haired dynamo who proudly showed him the roses he had never taken the time to smell.

Now, on the last day of their honeymoon, they drank in the rugged beauty of Blackwater Falls as the sound of the rushing water echoed loudly in their ears.

Trevor kept a possessive grip on Starr's arm as she watched the water breaking on the slippery stones below.

"I'm not going to fall in," she yelled at him as her blue eyes sparkled in the cold air.

Pulling her back from the precipitous edge, Trevor held her firmly in his arms. "I'm not taking any chances, Mrs. Hall," he said in her ear.

As his warm arms tightened around her, Starr smiled, lost in the beauty of the moment and the place. If anyone had ever told her she could be so happy with this impossible, mischievous, wonderful man, she wouldn't have believed it.

As they left the falls, Starr closed her eyes and said a silent prayer of thanksgiving.

Trevor's large hand covered hers and she smiled at him as a sense of shyness suddenly overcame her. It was still hard to believe he was really her husband.

"What were you thinking about with that 'cat-swallowed-the-canary' smile?"

"I was giving thanks."

He patted her hand in understanding and thought about the way his heart had thundered as he'd watched her come down the aisle on their wedding day. His hand had trembled so he could barely place the ring on her finger—not from fear, but from a blinding joy that consumed him. Starr, his beautiful Starr.

"So was I," he said quietly.

Snuggling beside him on the front seat in the car, she watched the passing scenery with great interest. "Back to work Monday," she commented as they passed a small general store.

"Uh—Starr," Trevor began, clearing his throat nervously, "there's something I have to tell you about the store."

"Oh?" Her blue eyes were wide in their innocence.

"About the lease on your store—"

"Yes?" she prompted.

"I'm the new landlord."

He waited for the explosion that didn't come. Her soft laughter filled the car. "I knew that."

At a loss for words, Trevor glanced at her in

amazement before looking back at the road.

"It wasn't that difficult to figure out, Trevor, darling. When Mr. Bowman wouldn't tell me and then Jan was so hush-hush, I knew it had to be you."

Trevor chuckled.

"Are you going to evict me? I think my lease is just about expired."

"I'll renew on one condition," he bargained.

"What condition?" Suspicion loomed in her eyes.

"When the first little Hall is born, you'll sell the store and be a full-time wife and mother."

After a short pause, she solemnly offered her hand.

"Deal," she agreed.

Trevor gave a long sigh of relief and pulled her against his shoulder.

"Lord, give me strength," he said with mock exasperation. "I'm facing a life of peanut butter sandwiches and sprouts."

Starr smiled as she nestled close to him, closing her eyes in happiness.

"You don't fool me, Trevor Hall," she murmured. "You're going to love every minute of it."

Smiling in complete agreement, Trevor turned the car homeward toward the rolling hills of Springfield.

Other Living Books Best-sellers

LORD, YOU LOVE TO SAY YES by Ruth Harms Calkin. In this collection of prayer-poems the author speaks openly and honestly with her Lord about hopes and dreams, longings and frustrations, and her observations of life. 07-3824 $2.95.

MORE THAN A CARPENTER by Josh McDowell. A hard-hitting book for people who are skeptical about Jesus' deity, his resurrection, and his claims on their lives. 07-4552 $2.95.

NOW IS YOUR TIME TO WIN by Dave Dean. In this true-life story, Dean shares how he locked into seven principles that enabled him to bounce back from failure to success. Read about successful men and women—from sports and entertainment celebrities to the ordinary people next door—and discover how you too can bounce back from failure to success! 07-4727 $2.95.

THE POSITIVE POWER OF JESUS CHRIST by Norman Vincent Peale. All his life the author has been leading men and women to Jesus Christ. In this book he tells of his boyhood encounters with Jesus and of his spiritual growth as he attended seminary and began his world-renowned ministry. 07-4914 $3.95.

REASONS by Josh McDowell and Don Stewart. In a convenient question-and-answer format, the authors address many of the commonly asked questions about the Bible and evolution. 07-5287 $3.95.

ROCK by Bob Larson. A well-researched and penetrating look at today's rock music and rock performers, their lyrics, and their lifestyles. 07-5686 $3.50.

SHAPE UP FROM THE INSIDE OUT by John R. Throop. Learn how to conquer the problem of being overweight! In this honest, often humorous book, Throop shares his own personal struggle with this area and how he gained fresh insight about the biblical relationship between physical and spiritual fitness. 07-5899 $2.95.

TAKE ME HOME by Bonnie Jamison. This touching, candid story of the author's relationship with her dying mother will offer hope and assurance to those dealing with an aging parent, relative, or friend. 07-6901 $3.50.

TELL ME AGAIN, LORD, I FORGET by Ruth Harms Calkin. You will easily identify with Calkin in this collection of prayer-poems about the challenges, peaks, and quiet moments of each day. 07-6990 $3.50.

THROUGH GATES OF SPLENDOR by Elisabeth Elliot. This unforgettable story of five men who braved the Auca Indians has become one of the most famous missionary books of all times. 07-7151 $3.95.

WAY BACK IN THE HILLS by James C. Hefley. The story of Hefley's colorful childhood in the Ozarks makes reflective reading for those who like a nostalgic journey into the past. 07-7821 $3.95.

Other Living Books Best-sellers

THE ANGEL OF HIS PRESENCE by Grace Livingston Hill. This book captures the romance of John Wentworth Stanley and a beautiful young woman whose influence causes John to reevaluate his well-laid plans for the future. 07-0047 $2.50.

HOW TO BE HAPPY THOUGH MARRIED by Tim LaHaye. One of America's most successful marriage counselors gives practical, proven advice for marital happiness. 07-1499 $3.50.

JOHN, SON OF THUNDER by Ellen Gunderson Traylor. In this saga of adventure, romance, and discovery, travel with John—the disciple whom Jesus loved—down desert paths, through the courts of the Holy City, to the foot of the cross. Journey with him from his luxury as a privileged son of Israel to the bitter hardship of his exile on Patmos. 07-1903 $4.95.

KAREN'S CHOICE by Janice Hermansen. College students Karen and Jon fall in love and are heading toward marriage when Karen discovers she is pregnant. Struggle with Karen and Jon through the choices they make and observe how they cope with the consequences and eventually find the forgiveness of Christ. 07-2027 $3.50.

LIFE IS TREMENDOUS! by Charlie "Tremendous" Jones. Believing that enthusiasm makes the difference, Jones shows how anyone can be happy, involved, relevant, productive, healthy, and secure in the midst of a high-pressure, commercialized society. 07-2184 $2.50.

LOOKING FOR LOVE IN ALL THE WRONG PLACES by Joe White. Using wisdom gained from many talks with young people, White steers teens in the right direction to find love and fulfillment in a personal relationship with God. 07-3825 $3.50.

LORD, I KEEP RUNNING BACK TO YOU by Ruth Harms Calkin. In prayer-poems tinged with wonder, joy, humanness, and questioning, the author speaks for all of us who are groping and learning together what it means to be God's child. 07-3819 $3.50.

SUCCESS: THE GLENN BLAND METHOD by Glenn Bland. The author shows how to set goals and make plans that really work. His ingredients of success include spiritual, financial, educational, and recreational balances. 07-6689 $3.50.

MOUNTAINS OF SPICES by Hannah Hurnard. Here is an allegory comparing the nine spices mentioned in the Song of Solomon to the nine fruits of the Spirit. A story of the glory of surrender by the author of *HINDS' FEET ON HIGH PLACES*. 07-4611 $3.50.

THE NEW MOTHER'S BOOK OF BABY CARE by Marjorie Palmer and Ethel Bowman. From what you will need to clothe the baby to how to know when to call the doctor, this book will give you all the basic knowledge necessary to be the parent your child needs. 07-4695 $2.95.

Other Living Books Best-sellers

ANSWERS by Josh McDowell and Don Stewart. In a question-and-answer format, the authors tackle sixty-five of the most-asked questions about the Bible, God, Jesus Christ, miracles, other religions, and creation. 07-0021 $3.95.

THE BEST CHRISTMAS PAGEANT EVER by Barbara Robinson. A delightfully wild and funny story about what happens to a Christmas program when the "Horrible Herdman" brothers and sisters are miscast in the roles of the biblical Christmas story characters. 07-0137 $2.50.

BUILDING YOUR SELF-IMAGE by Josh McDowell. Here are practical answers to help you overcome your fears, anxieties, and lack of self-confidence. Learn how God's higher image of who you are can take root in your heart and mind. 07-1395 $3.95.

THE CHILD WITHIN by Mari Hanes. The author shares insights she gained from God's Word during her own pregnancy. She identifies areas of stress, offers concrete data about the birth process, and points to God's sure promises that he will "gently lead those that are with young." 07-0219 $2.95.

400 WAYS TO SAY I LOVE YOU by Alice Chapin. Perhaps the flame of love has almost died in your marriage. Maybe you have a good marriage that just needs a little "spark." Here is a book especially for the woman who wants to rekindle the flame of romance in her marriage; who wants creative, practical, useful ideas to show the man in her life that she cares. 07-0919 $2.50.

GIVERS, TAKERS, AND OTHER KINDS OF LOVERS by Josh McDowell and Paul Lewis. This book bypasses vague generalities about love and sex and gets right to the basic questions: Whatever happened to sexual freedom? What's true love like? Do men respond differently than women? If you're looking for straight answers about God's plan for love and sexuality, this book was written for you. 07-1031 $2.95.

HINDS' FEET ON HIGH PLACES by Hannah Hurnard. A classic allegory of a journey toward faith that has sold more than a million copies! 07-1429 $3.95.

LORD, COULD YOU HURRY A LITTLE? by Ruth Harms Calkin. These prayer-poems from the heart of a godly woman trace the inner workings of the heart, following the rhythms of the day and the seasons of the year with expectation and love. 07-3816 $2.95.

WHAT WIVES WISH THEIR HUSBANDS KNEW ABOUT WOMEN by James Dobson. The best-selling author of *DARE TO DISCIPLINE* and *THE STRONG-WILLED CHILD* brings us this vital book that speaks to the unique emotional needs and aspirations of today's woman. An immensely practical, interesting guide. 07-7896 $3.50.

The books listed are available at your bookstore. If unavailable, send check with order to cover retail price plus $1.00 per book for postage and handling to:

Christian Book Service
Box 80
Wheaton, Illinois 60189

Prices and availability subject to change without notice. Allow 4–6 weeks for delivery.